Merry
SIGNPOSTS

33 tales

Corey Nash Small

Signposts

By

'The Tale Spinners'

Jake Corey * Linda Nash * Vesla Small

Best Wishes
Jake Corey (Laurie) LHC

Best wishes
Vesla Small (Else-Marie Amundsen)

Copyright © 2015 Corey, Nash and Small

All rights reserved.

ISBN 13 - 9781517053451

ISBN 10 - 1517053455

CONTENTS

	Foreword	
1	May In Bloom	Page 1
2	It's No Good Crying Over Spilt Milk	8
3	Fly Birdie, Fly!	14
4	Cuckoo In The Nest?	17
5	A Heroic Neighbour	25
6	Paradise Lost	29
7	Every Cloud	37
8	Mayday	44
9	Everyday Life	50
10	Mommy Clown	57
11	Simon	61
12	Prevention Is Better Than Cure	69
13	Just Do It	76
14	The Storm	84
15	Fortune And Misfortune	88
16	The Clock	97
17	The Albatross	105
18	Foreign Liaison	110
19	A Friend From The Past	115
20	The Lift	120
21	The Adventurer	129
22	The Tramp	135
23	The Prisoner	141
24	The Visit	148
25	Conversation With The Dead	155
26	Do As You Would Be Done By	165

27	A Stroke Of Luck	172
28	A Summer Romance	177
29	Use Your Gumption	181
30	The Prince And I	188
31	The Truth Behind The Myth	194
32	The Pond	199
33	Try To Forget	206

FOREWORD

We are *'The Tale Spinners'*. We are amateur writers, who enjoy writing and this book includes a small selection of our writing.

Our group meets each month. We choose a different theme for each meeting and members write a short story based on the theme. Before the next meeting, designated members review and critique our stories. To expand our horizons, we include a tribute to a writer, we also have writing tips and recently we've introduced a fifty-word story exercise.

These stories have been evaluated, edited, re-edited and proofread. Even so, they are not perfect. But they are the result of three years of writing by enthusiasts.

We decided to publish this book to raise money for a small but deserving children's charity. Our wish is to help it a little and hopefully to raise its profile.

We would like to thank Derek who designed and produced the cover.

1
MAY IN BLOOM
By Jake Corey

May in bloom, a fluffy sky and his 'Guardian' newspaper. What more could a man want? This is the life, he thought, sipping beer and skimming through the obituary column. Toby's in there, poor old sod. Suppose he'd have to go to the funeral the following week. Scanning the rest of the obituary list he smiled when he didn't spot his own name. That was good news.

He pondered his circumstances and concluded that there were worse ways to spend the time than waiting for Rosie, his wife. As far as he recalled, he'd always had to wait for her. This time it was shopping for a summer blouse.

They'd married in 1966, or was it 67? That summer they'd driven along the beach in a Volkswagen Beetle. But 67 had been even hotter. At the wedding, the back of his shirt was soaked by the time Rosie had strolled down the aisle, as casual as you like. Even though Rosie was half an hour late, she looked delicious. So it must have been 1967. A grin crossed his face at the thought. It was yesterday again. A week in Bognor and back to work in the factory.

The factory had occupied the whole of their working lives, him on the lathe and Rosie in accounts. She knew what he earned each week, even before payday. She joked, that was why she'd married him. They were paid by the number of pipes turned, and he was the fastest turner in the factory. Pulling his panama hat lower over his eyes, he leaned back in the wicker chair, opened the Guardian at the foreign news section then placed it over his face, and smiled.

Someone tapped him on the shoulder, waking him with a start, if it's Rosie, she's early, he thought. The waiter pointed to his empty beer glass and asked if he wanted another, then grinned as his Guardian made a spirited bid to escape. There was a time he might have chased after it, but he'd almost finished the paper and the sports section held no thrills. The thing fluttered like a flag let off the leash, then transformed into a bird of prey riding the thermals, the sun at its back. He refused the beer and prepared to settle again.

Before he could slump into the chair, he saw Rosie crossing the road, her cotton dress pressed against her legs by the light breeze. She strolled in his direction, holding her sun hat by the brim. He beamed, the same girl he'd married, with a touch of seasoning.

"Come on, lazy bones. Let's walk. It's a lovely day and we can't spend it sleeping," Rosie grinned reaching for his hand.

"No chance with you around," he mumbled and heaved himself out of the chair.

"We're so lucky with the weather this year. Like 76?"

"That was a year," he said.

"One to remember."

He shook his head. That was a heady summer. A hosepipe ban, fires on the Yorkshire moors, people dying of dehydration. The summer had been timelessly delicious. On their way to the coast, their Volkswagen had broken down just outside Happy Bottom in Dorset. Instead, they'd spent the weekend at a bed and breakfast they couldn't afford, called Bindon Bottom. They'd strolled along an endless path through the wood and travelled with an ageless stream making its fineless way seawards.

"We chose a name right then."

She smiled and squeezed his hand.

"Bluebell."

As they turned off the main street, Rosie pointed up, "Look, fantastic." With a little squeal she waved towards dozens of hot air balloons filling the sky. Light glinted off the canopies and passengers in the gondolas returned her wave.

"Where do you imagine they're going, dear?" he asked.

"Happy Bottom, I should think," she said, waving with the enthusiasm of a child.

She reached towards the galleons in the sky, as if she could touch them. To ensure he followed, she grasped his hand. It had always been that way. That's what he loved. She was the dreamer, he was practical.

"Let's follow," she said, pulling. "Come on, we'll miss them."

He followed her, as he'd always done, trailing at a trot. They turned into a field and she led him through a gate. More to himself than to Rosie, he mumbled, "Should we be doing this. We don't know who owns the field."

"I don't care. Hurry," she said.

Two black and white cows looked at them and went back to their mastication.

Even though the dozens of balloons were now pinpricks, she still waved. As they gained height, each disappeared, winking out like stars on a dark night. It may have been a hundred yard trot, but to his relief, Rosie slowed to a dawdle.

"Let's sit for a while, get our breath," she suggested, puffing and laughing.

During the summer of 76 there wasn't a wet field in the country and this was no different. He looked around for a spot to sit that looked free of anything that might spoil her dress. Even now, she didn't merely sit, but sank into the long grass with natural grace, his prima ballerina.

The field was a display of buttercups and daisies. Nature had laid on a spread, for them alone.

"I'm on buttercups, you're on daisies," Rosie announced.

"When was that?" he asked.

"Do you need to ask? It was 1982, spring. You must remember. A farmer and his bull chased us from his field. I've never seen you move so fast. The farmer caught us."

"He shook his fist then softened and let us stay the weekend."

That weekend they learned how to milk cows, muck out the goats and feed the chickens. After that, they bought a hen and a cockerel, two rabbits and a goat.

Rosie turned onto her front and spread her buttercups on the grass for him to examine.

"Get a move on, get picking," she laughed and gave him a nudge.

"Yes, mistress," he said, in mock servility, tipping the rim of his panama.

That's how our son got his name, after Nathaniel the farmer.

"Just think, if we'd had another girl, we'd have called her Daisy. She'd never have forgiven us."

He brushed her silver hair away from her eyes and stroked her cheek. Her lips brushed his hand with the tenderness of a bee testing the scent of a rose. He returned her osculation, brushing her cheek with his fingers.

"It's been a wonderful journey. More than any woman had a right to expect."

"Don't get all sentimental on me. Anyway, it's not over yet and you're cooking dinner tonight."

He gave her a bunch of daisies and closed his eyes. In seconds, she made the chain and slipped it into his shirt breast pocket. No doubt it would stay there until her next wash.

"Let's go to the park and I'll push you on the swings?" he suggested, pointing towards Clements Park.

"Not too fast, you're not a teenager," she teased.

"I'll have you know, I have the physique of Adonis," he said, striking a body builder's pose.

"Yes dear, but he's two and half thousand years old now. Come on, let's not waste the rest of the day. But gentle exercise, remember?"

Their fingers interlinked and they set off towards the park. He pointed out the pattern of the cirrocumulus clouds, shading his eyes.

"Look, there's five, no six dots of cloud, a domino."

Since the doctor had advised him to consider less active interests, he'd become something of an expert on clouds,

"Look, a fluffy one over there, a roller coaster. What's that?"

"That is stratocumulus. Fluffier you see, with specific shapes. That's not a rollercoaster, but a fire eating dragon. Talking of roller coasters, years ago you took the children on the roller coaster at Blackpool. Bluebell burst into tears but Nath loved it. It was weeks before she lived that down."

"Hmm. When was that then? Bluebell must have been eight something,… 84?"

"1985. 'Everyone Wants To Rule The World'. You kept singing it and we joined in. To us, it was the most beautiful song. Nath broke his collarbone on the sea slide and we waited in Accident and Emergency for hours. Nath kept the nurses busy asking for ice cream."

The park was empty, unusual for a summer afternoon.

"Come on, we have it to ourselves."

"Here, dear, take my bag will you?"

She sat on the swing, swung her legs and pushed off.

"Push," she demanded.

He helped by pushing the swing. The sun made sparkling waves of light and greys of shadow as she passed in front of its glare. Rosie pushed out her legs in front and leaned back. A young girl's enthusiasm and spirit in a loving wife's body. She was his strawberries and cream, his vintage champagne and the reason he'd survived his last heart attack.

"More," she squealed. "Don't stop, don't ever stop. Promise?"

She laughed, throwing her head back. Her hair flowed in the breeze. Once again, she was the twenty year old he'd married.

"I promise," he chuckled.

Chased by time's winged chariot, the swing eventually came to a halt. He held it steady as she slipped off.

"I enjoyed that. The park is all ours, let's paddle."

He took her bag, and they strolled over to the pond. She grasped his hand, pulling and encouraging. The ducks looked to them, perhaps expecting food. They sat on the concrete edge of the pond and slipped off their shoes. A brave duck plucked at his sock, then dropped it and flew off leaving a black feather. Rosie picked it up and tickled his toes with it.

"Keep it. For good luck," she said.

"Who says?" he challenged.

"I did. Let me put it in your hat."

She took his panama and pushed the feather behind the band.

Hands locked together as they stepped over the concrete rim and into the pond. Tip toes making dents in the water. The coldness defied the sun's warmth. It was cool and tingling as it crept up his shins. With his face turned to the sun, he felt the contrast of cold water and warm sun and said a silent thank you. His wife adopted the same pose, stretching out her arms, palms outstretched, catching the last rays. They stood in silence, in their own conjoined world. If this was their sculpture, it might have been called 'Convergence'.

It could have been minutes or more. His feet weren't cold, but he'd lost all feeling in them. She turned to face him and held both his hands in hers. Her eyes sparkled with images of the places they'd seen and shared. The curves of her body reflected their common experiences, both joys and disappointments. He saw in her eyes, the baby they'd lost and the miracle of their two wonderful children. Her smile showed trust and expectation, with an insistence she'd earned over decades. Understanding wasn't necessary, he accepted.

A siren brought him out of his reverie. He woke with a start. The sun was low and its fading light cast shadows of menacing proportions. Bluebell ran across the road towards him.

"Dad, dad. Mum's gone to hospital in an ambulance. A stroke, I think. She collapsed in a shop. You'd better come in my car."

Bluebell, the organiser, the level headed of the two. The one who until now, had always been so composed, was in danger of fragmenting. Bluebell's face was a mask of tears, pain and fear. He hugged her as she shook, racked with dread.

Bluebell took his hand and lead him to the car. On the way to the hospital, he touched the rim of his hat. The black feather was there. His hand went to his breast pocket. The buttercup and daisy chain was where his beautiful Rosie had left it. He smiled.

"Dad, are you alright?" Bluebell asked taking his hand.

"Yes love, I'm fine, and so is your mum."

2
IT'S NO GOOD CRYING OVER SPILT MILK
By Linda Nash

Felicity sat on the bed, dressed in pyjamas, thoughtfully chewing the end of her pen. An exercise book lay open on her lap, half filled with writing, or scribbling as her mother called it. She'd reached a point in her story, where she was finding it difficult to continue. She sighed and laid her exercise book and pen on the bed.

"Felicity," came her mother's voice from downstairs, "you realise that you have only half-an-hour before you must leave for school?"

Felicity gasped and looked at her watch, she had once again lost track of time and now she would have to rush. Felicity quickly pulled on some underwear and a pair of jeans. A tee shirt, denim jacket, socks and trainers, followed. She pulled a comb through her long fair hair, putting it into a ponytail, and following a glance in the mirror, she ran downstairs to the kitchen.

"Oh there you are," said her mother planting a quick kiss on her head, "come and eat your breakfast. I've made you some scrambled eggs. Is that okay?"

It wasn't, but Felicity didn't feel like arguing. Her small brother, Jonathan, was sitting at the end of the table, banging a wooden spoon as hard as he could on the tray in front of him. She kissed his brown curls and he gurgled in delight. "Flissie, kissie," he repeated, beaming at her with delight.

Felicity sat at the kitchen table, reflecting that it was rather a shame that Jonathan was so much younger than her. He was two years old to her eleven. She would have preferred having a brother nearer her own age, but she knew from friends at school, that when your parents divorced and married again, the likelihood was that any brothers or sisters would be a lot younger than you. Anyway, he was sweet, really.

Felicity quickly ate her breakfast, or as much of it as she could manage, put the rest in the bin and her plate in the dishwasher. She ran upstairs, rapidly brushed her teeth, grabbed her satchel, kissed her mother and Jonathan goodbye and ran out the door, just climbing on the school bus before it drew away from the kerb.

It was a normal day at school, the one interesting lesson being English, which was Felicity's best subject. Their teacher asked them to write a composition on something they had done during the school holidays. She wrote enthusiastically on a day she had spent with her father in London, where he lived. As she described the visit they'd made to the Foundling Museum in the morning, the delicious lunch at an Indian Restaurant and then shopping for her birthday present, she realised, once again, just how much she missed him. Felicity often wished she could go and live with him, but knew that this was impossible. Sophie, his new wife, worked full time for the same company as her father and couldn't look after her. When Felicity thought about Sophie, she realised that she didn't very much like her. It wasn't that she'd taken her father away, it was more that Felicity felt Sophie resented her, perhaps for occupying a special place in his affections.

Maybe now that Sophie was going to have a baby, things would be better between them. This led her on to thinking about George, her mother's new partner, with whom Felicity had a rather precarious relationship. Something else Felicity didn't understand was why her father had decided it was necessary to remarry and her mother didn't. According to her mother, her father didn't have a choice when he took up with Sophie. Felicity had noticed that although her mother often said nasty things about Sophie, Sophie never mentioned her mother. Felicity found the whole situation very confusing.

She handed in her composition at the end of the lesson, packed up her satchel and headed out for the school bus. She sat alone, not wishing to talk, trying to decide how she was going to end her story.

About ten minutes later she arrived home, opened the door and went into the kitchen, where her mother was giving Jonathan his tea. He waved a spoon in excitement when he saw Felicity.

"Flissie, Flissie."

She went over and kissed his cheek, trying to find a place that was not sticky with his tea. He beamed at her. She went over to her mother who was cooking dinner and kissed her. She thought her mother seemed a little preoccupied.

"I'm just going upstairs, Mummy," she said. "I want to finish my story."

"But, darling, have a drink, first and a piece of cake. It will be quite some time until supper, as George telephoned, to say he won't be home until seven o' clock."

Felicity sat at the kitchen table and drank the glass of apple juice, offered to her.

"I'll take the cake upstairs with me," she said. "I'm not hungry at the moment."

"Felicity," said her mother hesitantly, "I have something to say before you disappear upstairs. Something happened today, which, I am afraid, is going to upset you.

SIGNPOSTS

Jonathan got into your bedroom today and I am afraid he ..." she was unable to continue as Felicity leaped to her feet with a cry of anguish and raced upstairs to her bedroom.

Opening the door, she surveyed with horror what had been a reasonably tidy room when she had left for school. There were pieces of paper of varying sizes scattered everywhere, all torn from her precious exercise book, and they'd been scribbled on. She sat on the bed, looking around her in dismay. The only thing remaining whole was the cover. She sat there for a moment, stunned. Then suddenly she was overwhelmed with anger.

'This would never have happened before when Mummy and Daddy were together. Why couldn't her mother have been more careful? Jonathan was allowed to do whatever he wanted.

Tears of rage ran down her cheeks, as she tore down the stairs to the kitchen, where her mother was anxiously waiting.

"How could you have let him do that," she screamed angrily. "He's destroyed my story. It means starting all over again and it's impossible to remember it exactly. It's difficult enough living in this house. You spend all your time with him. I might as well be invisible, and now he's allowed to go into my room and destroy my things."

"But darling," protested her mother, "while I was cleaning your room the phone rang, so I had to answer it, and I'm afraid I forgot to close the door. I was away for about five minutes, but during this time he managed to get into your room. I do not spend all my time with him, but babies require more time than girls of your age. I must say I was a little surprised that you had left your things on your bed, you're usually meticulous about putting things away."

Felicity, however, was beyond reasoning.

"What," she shrieked, "are you saying it's my fault?" It was then that all the bitterness and anger she had kept to herself since her parents had split up welled up inside and

11

spilled over in a torrent of rage and unhappiness. Still sobbing, she ran out of the kitchen, up the stairs and into her room, slamming the door. Flinging herself on to the bed she lay looking up at the ceiling, wishing that things could go back to the way they were before her parents split up, conveniently pushing to the back of her mind the unhappiness that had pervaded the house.

Finally, she fell asleep emotionally exhausted and woke to hear a timid knocking on her bedroom door, and then her mother's voice.

"Supper's almost ready, love. Are you coming down?"

Felicity thought for a moment. "No thank you, I'm not hungry." In truth, she was starving, but did not intend to let her mother get off with things that lightly. She expected her mother to protest, but to her surprise, her mother went downstairs.

Eventually, her hunger pangs got the better of her and she reluctantly opened the bedroom door and started to go downstairs. She stopped, on hearing her stepfather's voice.

"Oh leave her darling. Going without one meal won't do her any harm and she'll soon realise that all this crying and fuss over her story is a waste of time. She'll simply just have to sit down and write it again. Talk about crying over spilt milk. Jonathan didn't do it deliberately. After all, he's only two years' old."

Felicity couldn't believe her ears. She raced upstairs and slammed her bedroom door.

That did it. She could no longer live here. She'd have to go and live with her father whether Sophie liked it or not.

She took her mobile from her satchel. Her parents had agreed that she was only allowed to use it for emergencies, but if this wasn't an emergency, then what was? She opened her phone book and pressed her father's number.

Her father's mobile rang and rang. Felicity was just about to hang up when she heard his voice.

"Felicity what's happened. Why are you ringing?"

On hearing her father's voice, Felicity dissolved into

tears. Between sobs, she tried to explain what had happened, what her mother and stepfather had said and the injustice that had been done to her.

There was a long silence when she finished speaking.

"What do you want me to do about it, Fliss?"

Felicity couldn't believe her ears. Did her father not understand what had happened? How this meant that it was impossible for her to continue living here. Why was he not asking if she wanted to come and stay? Suddenly, she realised. She closed her phone and slowly returned it to her satchel.

From that short phrase, her father had made it obvious that she could not go and stay with him and his precious Sophie. Obviously, taking her out for the day or a weekend stay was one thing, but anything more long term was not a possibility. Felicity sighed. What was she going to do? Indeed, what could she do? Running away was hardly an option, because where would she go? Her Granny or Aunt Alice were the only possibilities and they would immediately contact her mother. She realised at that moment that she had no choice. Her home was here, in this house, with her mother, stepfather and baby Jonathan, whether she liked it or not. Her relationship with her father was no longer full time, but just on an occasional basis. 'High days and holidays,' just like her Granny said.

Felicity sighed again, got off her bed, opened the door and went into the bathroom, where she washed away all traces of her tears and combed her hair. Before going downstairs, she looked at herself in the mirror. Somehow, she looked older. She certainly felt it. It must have been the realisation of how her life was going to be. Pulling her shoulders back and holding her head high, she pushed open the bathroom door and walked slowly down the stairs to face her family.

3
FLY BIRDIE, FLY!
By Vesla Small

Once upon a time, there was a small boy and a baby robin.

It was a lovely day in June. A warm, pleasant breeze caressed the child's skin and blew his hair. It had been a lively morning, with both human and wildlife in the garden. The trees cast shadows in the afternoon sun. A butterfly fluttered its colourful wings and flew from one rose to another. The bees were busy pollinating the bright yellow honeysuckle blossoms.

With unsteady and eager steps, the toddler ran down the garden path, looking for the nest box in the tree. He helped his mum to fill the big water basin, and watched the birds bathe in it, keeping their plumage clean and fresh. Well fed neighbour cats also drank from the water and seemed to ignore the birds. The boy was impatient to see if the fledglings were ready to leave their nest.

On this special day, a young robin was getting ready to take off for the first time and the tot beamed, his eyes sparkling.

"Come on birdie. Be careful," said the little fellow, quietly.

The bird tweeted away. It moved its head up and down, ruffled its feathers, flapped its wings and prepared for takeoff.

"Fly birdie, fly!" the boy called out, in anticipation.

Suddenly, the robin 'threw' itself out of the nest, flapped its wings vigorously in fear for a short time, and steered towards the cherry tree where it landed on a twig thick with blossoms.

"Again birdie, again," the child exclaimed, and clapped his hands with joy.

The robin lifted off from the branch and flew in a circle above its spectator's head.

'I wish I could fly in the sky like a bird. I would fly to the sun and look down on the wood. I would sing beautiful songs, look for food and wear a soft feather coat to keep the cold out,' thought the boy, as he watched the robin.

'I wish I had legs and could walk in the grass without being threatened by cats, squirrels and cars. When a storm approaches or winter is close, I'd be dry and warm inside the house,' the bird thought, flapping its wings faster.

Then, the bird plummeted into the grass in front of the toddler. The young ones looked at each other. One seemed frightened, and the other was startled. Sadly, the robin appeared to have injured its wing and could fly no more.

The boy carefully lifted the bird and carried it to his mother.

"Mummy, birdie needs help."

They found a cage in the shed where the bird stayed safely until its wing healed. The boy fed the robin with insects and worms from the garden, making it healthy, strong and ready for its next takeoff.

Soon, it was time to free the robin, so early one morning the child stood with his mother, high on the veranda, with the bird in his hands. As he kissed it, he whispered, "Bye bye, birdie."

By now, the fledgling had grown into a bigger and stronger bird, and lifted off into the air and flew in a circle above its friend.

With tears in his eyes, the boy called, "Fly birdie, fly!"

As it sang a happy tune, it headed for the nearest cherry tree, with luscious cherries to feed on.

Some months later, it was almost Christmas time and Jack Frost had 'painted' the vegetation with his glorious silver white paint, when a robin, with its orange-red breast and throat, pecked at the kitchen windowpane, where the child ate his breakfast.

'It's the same bird with the speckled plumage we rescued last summer,' he thought.

"Mummy, birdie's back!" He sounded excited.

They fetched seeds and kibbled peanuts from the pantry. When the child came outside, the robin flew in circles above his head, moved his tail up and down, and sang. With his hand filled with birdfeed, the small boy watched the robin pecking at the food. All the while, the robin kept his beady eyes on the boy. After a while, it settled on the feeding table, and pecked greedily at the food.

"Little robin, I've missed you. Where were you?" he asked, looking happy.

"It was unsafe in your garden, so I moved to the other side of the road. In the garden where I live now, the cat wears a bell, so I can hear her when she comes," the robin chirped back.

"The road's busy. I'm afraid to cross it, so, I can't visit you," answered the boy.

"I'll perch on a bough in the highest fir tree, and when you're alone, I'll sing you a tune," chirped the robin.

And this is how it came about that robin redbreast continues to sing its cheerful melody, not caring much whether it's winter or spring.

4
CUCKOO IN THE NEST?
By Linda Nash

It was Spring again, bringing to mind gently budding, brightly coloured tulips, trees and bushes. A pale yellow sun hovered over them, giving out just enough warmth to germinate seeds, and encouraging plants to shyly push their leaves through the earth. Gentle showers of rain dampening the warming ground complete this idyllic picture. But that was the Spring of childhood memories, unmatched by reality.

Jennifer had spent the past week trying to get into the garden. The garden was her new passion, it had replaced work when she retired. She'd thought she would miss work and had never imagined that something so pedestrian as gardening could replace her exciting job in advertising. She'd faced retirement with some reluctance, although at 65 there was little choice. It was her husband, Peter, a rather unenthusiastic gardener when it came to flowers and totally devoid of any interest when it came to vegetables, who had surprised her one morning at breakfast,

"Darling, how would you feel about taking over some of the gardening when you leave work?" Retirement was not a word either of them employed as this hinted at the delicate subject of age, that is getting older.

Jennifer put down her toast, chewing the last mouthful thoughtfully.

"I'll think about it," she said carefully, not wishing to commit herself to something she might regret later and, more importantly, something from which she might not be able to extract herself. However, the following day while reading her newspaper on the train, she pondered on his suggestion and turned on impulse to the gardening page. It was full of suggestions as to what you could grow as regards flowers and vegetables and what you should be achieving this very week. Jennifer was staggered. Jennifer and Peter's idea of a garden was limited to grass requiring infrequent mowing, a few shrubs and a little weeding, all done with the help of a local gardener. Flowers and vegetables had never entered their realm of thought.

A few days later while lunching with her friend Petra, Jennifer told her what Peter had suggested and Petra looked her in astonishment.

"Do you think it's your thing," she said doubtfully, looking at Jennifer's perfectly manicured hands, smart clothes and carefully arranged hair, trying to replace them with old, worn clothes, wellington boots and gardening gloves.

"I really don't know," said Jennifer truthfully, "but I shall look into it."

And look into it she did. Replacing her daily newspaper with gardening magazines, Jennifer read avidly. She watched gardening programmes on television and visited gardens that were open to the public, and began to realise what a fascinating subject gardening was. When it came to her birthday, she asked Peter if he would pay for her to go on a gardening course, so that she could be taught by a professional how to garden. Peter, who always had problems in deciding what to buy for Jennifer's birthday, agreed, but he did wonder what he had unleashed with his tentative suggestion that she should help with the gardening.

At her leaving party at the end of March, Jennifer was presented with, thanks to Petra's intervention, several items befitting a future gardener. To date, she had not as yet actually ventured into the garden to practise some of her new found knowledge. She was still most definitely at the theoretical stage. Her office presented her with a year's subscription to the Royal Horticultural Society, a stainless steel trowel and fork in a wooden box, a lady's garden spade and fork and a very smart pair of green wellies. Jennifer was delighted and thanked everyone enthusiastically. The Director of the firm wished her a happy retirement and many hours of fulfilment in what was going to be her chosen retirement activity, although he, privately, shared Petra's doubts as to the suitability of Jennifer's chosen path.

The following day, Wednesday, the first day of her retirement, Jennifer woke up at her usual time, 6.30 a.m. She leaped out of bed, but instead of rushing into the shower, put on her dressing gown and slippers and wandered downstairs, where she put on the coffee. Jennifer looked out of the window to see what the weather was like. Much to her disappointment there was a light drizzle, not at all the type of weather in which to start her gardening career. However, as she sipped her coffee she thought this might be a good opportunity to visit the local Garden Centre to choose a few flowering plants to put around the shrubs. Simon came downstairs dressed for work and she gave him a cup of coffee. He looked at her, a worried expression on his face.

"You're not going to be too lonely on your own?" he said, a trace of anxiety in his voice. "Have you decided what you're going to do today?"

"Yes, replied Jennifer, "as it's raining I think I'll go and look round the Garden Centre for some flowering plants and maybe they'll have some information on possible gardening courses."

Following Simon's departure for the office, Jennifer showered, dressed in a smart pair of jeans, a warm checked shirt and puffa, and donned her new green boots. Before leaving, she examined herself in the mirror, nodding with approval at the gardener, who looked back at her. It took her ten minutes to get to the Gardening Centre and she arrived as it opened. However, an hour later she was still wandering around amongst the bewildering array of flowers and plants for sale, not having the slightest idea what or how many she should purchase. Suddenly, she realised that someone was speaking to her.

"I wonder if I can be of any assistance," said the voice. Turning around Jennifer saw a rugged, rather good looking man, in his early fifties, considerably taller than her. There was something familiar about him, which she couldn't quite place. When he smiled she noticed how blue his eyes were. Jennifer, not unlike the drowning man, gratefully accepted his offer. She started to explain her project, but he interrupted her

"Why don't we go to the cafe and you can tell me more over a cup of coffee?"

She readily agreed and they made their way through the many aisles of the Garden Centre, to arrive eventually at the small but welcoming cafe. Her saviour turned to her smiling,

"Is a coffee okay? By the way I'm Paul."

"I'm Jennifer and yes a coffee, black, would be perfect." Paul turned to the young woman manning the coffee machine.

"Two black coffees, please. Would you like something to eat?"

"Thank you, no," said Jennifer quickly, looking longingly at the array of delicious looking cakes and scones, but not wishing to appear either opportunistic or greedy.

The young woman behind the counter handed over the coffees.

"Here we are, Mr. Jackson."

Oh, thought Jennifer, so he must be the owner, but where had she heard that name before. She racked her brain and then suddenly it came to her, that perfectly tedious party at the Leighton Jones's house. It was he who had landscaped their garden so beautifully. The drinks party had been to show off their garden and, of course, he'd been there, but she'd not had the chance to talk to him. But then she remembered that at that time she had still been working in marketing and so a landscape gardener, or any gardener come to that, would not have been considered appropriate to her life.

They sat down at a corner table. Jennifer sipped at her coffee, feeling a little self-conscious and embarrassed at her rather snobbish recollection. Then Paul smiled encouragingly and once again she noticed the intense blue of his eyes and the friendliness of his smile.,

"Now tell me about your project and I can see where and how I can help you."

Jennifer, hesitantly told him about her project from the beginning, finishing lamely with, "I expect you think I'm rather silly and that my project is far too ambitious for somebody who has no experience of gardening."

"Not at all, "Paul said smiling at her, "but I do think you will need some help and perhaps some instruction as you have never really gardened before. If you wish, I could come to your house and give you hands on instruction while we plant. Or perhaps you have already found an instructor."

Jennifer smiled, feeling guilty on feeling so relieved that Simon had neither found a course nor a suitable instructor. But what was she thinking? This had to be on an official basis.

"You must let me know how much you charge for lessons."

He looked at her searchingly, "But of course. When would you like to start? How about the day after tomorrow? I have two hours free from 10 until 12."

Without a moment's hesitation, Jennifer accepted.

Thanking him effusively, she left the Garden Centre walking on air. The sun was shining and wasn't that a cuckoo she could hear in the distance. It was the first time she ever remembered having heard one. What a beautiful sound. Everything looked different. This project was turning out to be much more interesting than she could ever have imagined. Retirement was looking really exciting. She spent the rest of the day in a state of euphoria, coming to earth with a start when she heard Simon's key in the lock.

"How was your day?" he asked hesitantly.

"Okay," she said, "nothing very exciting. The Garden Centre was a bit disappointing, but I have managed to find an instructor. I'll have to see if he is any good though!"

Simon was delighted to see Jennifer in such good spirits. Although he had said nothing to her he had secretly worried about her transition from full time work to retirement. After all, she had put everything into her work when they had discovered that they would be unable to have children and now had to adapt to a life of leisure from a highly pressured working environment. Admittedly it was only the first day, but so far so good.

Tuesday, in stark contrast to Monday dawned fair. Jennifer rose early, made herself the obligatory cup of coffee and planned her day. She would start by weeding the beds, which contained only shrubs, and prepare the ground for flowers. Waving Simon off to work at eight o'clock, followed by a quick shower, Jennifer dressed herself in her gardening clothes, and gathered together her newly acquired tools and went into the garden. It was difficult to know where to start, every bed not only contained shrubs but every other inch of space was filled with weeds. Jennifer quailed inwardly, but this was not an acceptable attitude for a future successful gardener. Bracing herself, she put her kneeler into position by the bed nearest to the front door, took her fork in her right hand and plunged it into the ground near a particularly large dandelion. She then pulled hopefully on the dandelion, which obligingly broke off short. Jennifer was not to be pipped at the first post and dug deeply into the soil around where the dandelion had broken off. After several minutes of digging and probing she finally pulled out the offending root.

It came to her that perhaps gardening was not going to be as easy as she had first imagined.

After two hours of hard weeding, Jennifer was exhausted and she had cleared only one flowerbed. Every muscle in her body ached and she decided that a coffee break was called for. As she drank her coffee she felt her strength and determination return. After all, she had actually cleared one flowerbed, which was one more than she had previously done. She took a deep breath and returned to the garden determined to succeed. After all, she had overcome numerous hurdles and crises in her work, so there was no reason why she could not overcome them now.

By four o'clock Jennifer was done. No, she had not weeded the entire garden, she could only lay claim to having weeded two flowerbeds, but she reminded herself, this was after all her first attempt at weeding. It had started drizzling again, so she decided to give up and go inside.

As she got to her feet she realised her whole body was one big ache. Nothing that a hot bath will not cure, she told herself. Fortunately, she had bought herself some special bath lotion for gardeners. That should do the trick. After diligently soaking her aching body for an hour, she gave up and decided that she had most probably overdone her first full day in the garden.

By the time Simon came home at around 7 p.m. all she really wanted was to give way to her aching body and lie down and rest. Simon was horrified when he saw her and asked whether she shouldn't cancel her lesson for the following day.

But Jennifer was made of sterner stuff. She was sure that she would be fully recovered by the following day. Just the thought of taking lessons in gardening from the ruggedly handsome man from the Gardening Centre made her recovery a certainty.

5
A HEROIC NEIGHBOUR
By Vesla Small

The ship shuddered as waves smashed above the ship. Anna's decision to travel had seemed sensible, but now she wished she'd listened to her husband's advice.

They'd planned this trip since Christmas and finally the day of departure had arrived. The children had school holidays and looked forward to the sea voyage and the wedding party.

***

"Shall, shall not, shall, shall not... Shall!" they shouted excitedly, counting the buttons on the shirt.

The tickets were bought, and a cabin was booked on the deck of the coastal liner, 'Northern Star'. This was the first time they would travel on a ship and they were excited even though there could be a complication. The weatherman had announced a heavy storm over the West Fjord.

"Shall!" they pleaded.

"It'll be rough, and you'll get seasick," their father advised, a look of concern crossing his face.

"No, no, we won't," they sounded excited and adamant.

Despite her husband's warning, Anna decided to make the journey. The children waved eagerly to their father from the taxi, on their way to the harbour.

As they ran up the gangplank, with rucksacks on their backs, the ship's Captain saluted the siblings. The children jumped in surprise at the sound of the ship's horn and laughed. Installed in the small cabin, they peeped through the porthole, as passengers walked past on the deck. The long awaited sea voyage had begun, and this would be their 'home', for the next thirty-six hours.

A neighbour, Arthur, was also on the ship and had been a sailor all his life. He offered to show them around, and since he knew the Captain, they were invited to visit the bridge. When the Captain showed them the helm with its controls for steering and engine power, Arthur ruffled the boy's hair, and laughed, "You'll be an expert in navigation by the time you leave the ship."

Whilst the grownups sat on deckchairs on the afterdeck and talked, the boy continued running around while his sister hung her head over the railing, looking pale.

Dark clouds appeared on the horizon. Arthur looked at Anna, and said, "It looks like the weather forecast's correct. I hope you've brought medication for travel sickness. This will be a rough crossing."

"No, Arthur, I didn't. Do you have any?" Anna asked.

He fumbled around in his rucksack until he found what he was looking for. "Swallow one pill with water and it'll take effect within less than half an hour."

Even before they'd settled in their bunk-beds, the boat rocked on the rough sea. The ship had entered the West Fjord, and the crossing would take four hours. Through the porthole, they saw the wild waves, topped with white foam, thrown against the side of the ship. It looked impressive. Finally, they fell asleep.

SIGNPOSTS

***

"Man overboard!"

'Is it a dream or is it real?' Anna asked herself, drugged with sleep,

It was real. The ship had come to a halt. Anna heard people run and shout, and through the porthole, she watched the crew struggle to lower a lifeboat over the side of the ship, in the crashing waves.

Anna told the children to stay in the cabin, whilst she went out to find her bearings. Feeling the cold, she wrapped up, before she left the cabin, and rushed to the deck.

The ship's lanterns illuminated the deck and the mountainous sea. Anna could see the shadow of Arthur on deck, preparing to board the lifeboat, with a line attached to his life vest.

"Throw the line. Now!" someone shouted.

The men lowered the lifeboat with Arthur on board. The storm looked angry, and the lifeboat looked like a leaf riding the raging waves.

'That's not for the faint hearted,' thought Anna, stunned by the power of the sea and its gigantic waves, fearful for Arthur's life.

The wind whipped the sea spray into her face, her anorak hood flying off. Anna clung to the railing on the inner part of the deck, on the lookout for the lifeboat.

"Something's over there!" someone shouted and pointed out to sea.

Anna was relieved that Arthur appeared to master the steering of the lifeboat. She watched her neighbour throw a lifebuoy towards the man overboard.

'Will he catch the lifebuoy?' Anna fretted.

The crowd on the deck watched Arthur leaving the boat and thrust himself in the direction of the sinking man. Both disappeared beneath the waves, but to Anna's relief, she saw Arthur hang on to the side of the lifeboat with one hand, while with the other he gripped the man in distress, looking lifeless.

Arthur pushed the body into the lifeboat and hoisted himself on board the rocking boat. The crew pulled on the line to haul the lifeboat back to the ship in the raging sea.

Whilst passengers and crew shouted, "Keep pulling! Almost there!" Arthur showed his death defying skills.

'Thank God, he's safe,' thought Anna.

She thought about her father, who'd been a fisherman all his life. She'd always admired his resourcefulness as fisherman, and his ability to judge the weather, the sea and his vessel. Had he been alive, he would most likely have given her the same advice as her husband.

The exhausted men received blankets and warm drinks, and the ship's doctor attended to them. The storm had calmed down by the time the ship anchored at the next harbour where an ambulance waited for the rescued man.

No one had expected such remarkable deeds from Arthur, an ordinary person. In fact, he was an extraordinary man, prepared to sacrifice his life for someone else's.

Later, when Anna met Arthur, he said, "It was strange. The man I rescued was my cabin companion. I dared not think about the alternative."

6
PARADISE LOST
By Linda Nash

It was a beautiful summer morning. The sky was a pale blue, with the occasional trace of a wispy cloud and the sun was already warm, promising another hot day. Apart from birdsong and the muffled sound of a distant train, all was silent. Susan relaxed, inhaling deeply the fresh early morning air. She walked slowly through the wood, Sam, her Golden Retriever, bounded ahead, his enthusiasm for his early morning walk showing in his bright eyes, cocked ears and wagging tail. He ran through the trees, pushing impatiently through the undergrowth, until his mistress could no longer see him.

Both of them loved this time together in the early mornings. It was rarely that they met anybody, it was as though the countryside belonged only to them.

"Oh, if only this could go on forever," thought Susan. "When I think that I must return to that boring office in a week's time."

She pushed this unwelcome thought to the back of her mind, enjoying instead the sunlight softly dappling the leaves, the contrasting colours surrounding her; the varying greens and yellows of new foliage, which would in a few months look brown, dry and parched. She loved this season of new life. Susan had passed, on her way to the wood, young calves, newly born and still dependent on their mothers. Their soft, brown eyes had looked up at her, their beauty and innocence reminding her why she no longer cared to eat meat. Susan reflected on her good fortune in living in this rural part of England, with its rolling, wooded countryside, dotted with small towns and villages and its beautiful rugged coastline.

Lost in happy thoughts, Susan was rudely awakened by the sound of frantic barking, somewhere to her right. She quickened her pace, pushing her way through clumps of nettles and ferns, still, fortunately low to the ground. In another six weeks they would be almost as tall as she was.

"Thank goodness I didn't wear shorts."

The barking sounded nearer, and then in a small clearing ahead she could just make out Sam bounding around.

As she approached, she realised that he was jumping up at something. Susan cursed herself for once again forgetting her glasses. She called to Sam,

"Calm boy, I'm coming."

Sam, who was an obedient dog in normal circumstances, took no notice, but continued turning in frenzied circles, barking noisily.

As she drew nearer, she realised in horror why he was not obeying her commands.

"Oh my God," she gasped, swallowing a scream, which threatened to overwhelm her. She shut her eyes, counted to ten and then slowly opened them, hoping that she'd been mistaken, or that it was some terrible dream from which she would wake. But no, it was still there that limp body hanging from the tree. To her horror, she realised that there was something horribly familiar about it.

"Oh but it can't be," she whispered. "It's Chris that young boy from the Close."

She ran into the bushes and was violently sick. She felt

cold and was shivering violently. Somehow she managed to get her mobile telephone out of her pocket, and her hand shaking, she dialled 999. There was an immediate response, did she want police, fire or ambulance. She hesitated, wanting both police and ambulance, but she opted for police as she was reporting a crime and, no doubt, they would call for an ambulance, if it was required.

"Cranchester police, here. Can I help you?"

"Yes," she said, taking a deep breath while trying hard to regain some composure.

"I was walking in Gately woods on the path which starts just outside Cranchester and I am now standing in a clearing about half a mile into the woods and approximately 100 yards to the right of the central path. My dog has found a young man hanging from one of the trees. His Christian name is Chris, but I'm afraid I don't know his surname. He lives in Thisby Close, which is just off Gateley Road, where I live."

"Just stay where you are, Miss. Your name?"

"It's Susan Stockley. Yes, I will stay here, but please come quickly, won't you? I'm feeling dreadful. I'm very cold and can't stop shaking."

"Don't worry, Miss Stockley. We will be there right away. Meanwhile, sit down, with your back to the body."

Susan did as she was told and sat hugging Sam, who seemed to understand that what she needed was comfort and warmth.

After a short wait she became aware of the sound of a vehicle slowly making its way along the footpath. When she estimated that it was more or less level to where she was sitting, she stood up and shouted.

"Over here."

Two policemen and one policewoman came towards her through the undergrowth. Seeing them, her composure left her and she started crying and shivering. The policewoman, carrying a blanket, came over to her. She wrapped it around Susan and then produced a thermos from her bag and poured her a cup from its contents.

"Drink this, love," she said, "it's hot and sweet and it will calm you and warm you at the same time."

Susan huddled into the blanket, slowly sipping the sweet tea. She started to feel slightly better.

Meanwhile, the two policemen were examining the body.

"Better not do anything until forensics get here," said the younger of the two.

"They should be here in about fifteen minutes," said the other, "they've got to come from Whitmouth. How's the young lady doing?"

"She's in shock and quite cold. I'll take her to the car where she can sit down. You come too," this time she addressed Sam, who as if understanding the gravity of the situation, was sitting quietly by Susan's side.

The young policewoman, called Janet, helped Susan, whose legs were threatening to buckle beneath her, to the car, where another blanket was produced, into which she huddled gratefully. She shut her eyes and then opened them again to blot out the image that had appeared behind her closed lids. She shuddered in spite of the warm blankets.

"Are you alright love," Janet said softly, her concern evident.

"I can't stop seeing him. Every time I shut my eyes." Susan shuddered again. Sam licked her arm, looking up at his mistress anxiously.

"It won't be long now. I think I can hear a Police car. It must be the team from forensics. You stop here, and I will ask them if I can take you home. They'll want to talk to you later, but I'm sure they won't want you to hang around here."

Janet opened the car door and addressed one of the policemen who had arrived in the Police car. He looked over at Susan and nodded his agreement.

Janet returned to the van, got into the driving seat and

turned to Susan.

"I'm going to take you home now. You too," she said, smiling at Sam. "Inspector Caddy will come and see you at home later on. I'll give you his telephone number in case you need to go out."

Susan smiled weakly. She didn't think that she would be going out again today, or for the next few days, for that matter. All she wanted to do was go to bed and put her head under the bedclothes.

On the drive home, Susan stared out the window, taking comfort from the warmth of Sam, who sat on the seat next to her. The countryside was a blur of greens and browns, as they passed and soon, almost too soon, Janet drew up in front of Susan's house. She walked around the car and opened the door. Sam bounded out and Susan climbed out behind him, hardly trusting her legs. Janet accompanied them to the front door, taking the key from Susan when she saw how her hands were trembling. She held the door open for her and followed her into the house.

"Shall I make you a cup of tea?" she asked anxiously."

"No, I think I would prefer a cup of coffee. Let me make it, I need something to do."

Concentrating hard, she took down the tin of coffee with great care, she washed out the coffee pot, filled it with water, put in the coffee and then screwed the top back on. Gripping it with shaking hands, she placed it on the stove and then lit the stove.

"I'll make us some toast to go with the coffee."

She busied herself with cutting the bread, toasting it and taking the butter and jam from the fridge, trying to think only of what she was doing, not letting her mind slip back to those terrible images of less than an hour ago.

When the coffee was ready, Susan served it, together with the toast, butter and jam. Janet and Susan sat in silence for a few minutes. Susan ate, chewing every mouthful with care, trying to push away the nauseous feelings in her stomach. But it was no good. She leaped to her feet and rushed to the downstairs toilet, bringing up what little she had managed to eat.

Janet came over to her.

"Who's your Doctor? I'm going to call him," she said. Susan found the number on her telephone, dialled it and handed the phone to Janet.

When Janet got through, she explained to the Doctor what had happened and the urgency of the situation.

"He'll be along in about half an hour," she told Susan. "While we're waiting, I'll feed your dog."

When the doorbell rang, Janet went to the door. Dr. Phelps, who was almost a stranger to Susan, so rarely did she visit him, looked concerned. He took her blood pressure, frowned at the result, and told her that she needed to take something to cope with the shock and distress from which she was suffering. As if realising that she was about to protest, he added that she would only need to take the tablets for a short time, probably a few days.

Susan thanked him, but he patted her on the shoulder and said there was no need.

"Do you need a sick certificate, as I think you should stay at home for several days?"

She assured him she had a week's holiday remaining, so would not need a certificate, but that if there was a problem, she would come and see him at the surgery.

"There is no need for that. I shall be coming to check on you at the end of the week.

Janet let him out and then turned to Susan.

"Give me the prescription. I will pop down to the chemist and get it for you."

Susan turned to the side table where her purse lay.

"No, pay me when I get back," said Janet and laid a hand on Susan's.

Susan sank back gratefully on the couch and closed her eyes. This was ridiculous, she had to pull herself together.

The next thing she knew, Janet was gently shaking and asking her to take two tablets with a glass of water. She swallowed them down while Janet made some more toast. This she ate with small sips of water and to her relief it stayed down. Susan reached for her purse.

'How much do I owe you?'

"£5.60, and I will have to return to the Station now. Are you going to be okay? Anyway, I shall be back later this afternoon with the others, as they'll need to talk to you. You rest now and don't answer the door or the telephone. People can leave a message if they need to speak to you."

"I'm starting to feel a little better now. Thank you for everything."

"Don't mention it. It's all part of the job. I'll let myself out and will probably be back with the others around 1700."

After Janet had left, Susan remained lying on the couch and soon drifted off to sleep. Sam stayed by her side and did not move until he heard a knock on the door. Susan woke with a start, looking at her watch. It must be the Police as it was 1700. She had been asleep for hours.

She jumped to her feet, realising that she felt much stronger, and went to the door.

"Who is it?"

"It's Janet with Sergeant Caddy and Inspector Shaw."

Susan opened the door, while holding Sam's collar and let them in.

"Please come in. A cup of tea?"

"I'll get it," said Janet, "while you talk with the Inspector and the Sergeant."

Inexplicably, Susan felt very nervous and started to tremble. She sat down as her legs gave way.

The Inspector spoke to her in a low voice, trying to reassure her.

"Susan, may I call you by your Christian name? We only want to hear from you exactly what happened this morning."

Susan swallowed hard and began to speak, concentrating hard on every word.

"I went out early this morning, for a walk with Sam, my dog. I decided to go to the woods, as it was such a beautiful day ..." She tailed off, as she remembered how lovely the countryside looked under the early morning sunlight. A perfect day in the making. A fleeting glimpse of Paradise. How good she had felt, and then! She felt the tears start, as she recalled the dreadful moment when she discovered the body.

7
EVERY CLOUD
By Jake Corey

Press conferences are not for the faint hearted. In five years I've attended enough to last a lifetime. They're all here, from the gutter press to the highbrow, and I love and hate them. My mind's not in turmoil, it's straight. They got me bang to rights, as they say. Caught with my trousers over my arm but nothing up to my waist. That was a pity, another minute and I'd have been clean away.

I've been told to treat the press nicely, so I will, to a point. I've dressed for them. Jacket, that is, the whole works. I had to borrow a tie though. It's yellow, not my colour, but beggars and all that.

I wouldn't mind, but the bird didn't complain, not until her husband got hold of her, then she shouted

"It was his fault, flashing his money, got me drunk," prattling on as if her life depended on it and by the look on her husband's face, it did.

The public relations friend, next to me, digs me in the ribs and nods at the statement in which I say 'sorry', it was a single lapse. They were all 'single lapses' weren't they?

As I read the statement in my best contrite voice, I tell them the agreed line that my wife will stand by me. I glance in her direction, she's smiling. I wipe my hand across my mouth and feel a slight wetness on my top lip.

As I finish my statement, my press guy answers questions. Thank goodness that's finished. Now I put on a sorry expression, no problem. These days, footballers are better at acting than George Clooney. We have to be convincing. I grin but hide it behind my hand.

I smile demurely back at my wife, we're one happy family. She'd slip a knife between my ribs if she could, but I promised to give her everything for a 'no fault' divorce.

It's a good job she don't know about the others I didn't admit to. I spread my legs under the table and smile across at her, trying to look confident. I pop a chewing gum and throw a wink in her direction. She beams back with an 'I love you' grin.

Bloody hell, she hasn't got a private dick has she? No, she can't, no time. That's an evil grin on her mug. The press guy says it's over and I should thank the press.

"Thank you, I'm sorry," again, I think to myself. Like hell I am. I can hear myself spouting that me and my beautiful wife Sara who I'm in love with, need space to work out our future. She nods and I get up to leave. She walks across, grabs my hand and smiles, the adoring wife. I see a slight narrowing of her eyes, that's her tell.

Sara fixes my eyes and whispers. "I know about the bank accounts, you bastard."

I fix a British Airways smile but I have a hunch that the game's up, my legs shake.

Driving home in separate cars was like a slow walk to the gallows; too slow, too fast. Not enough time to think, but enough to get paranoid. Paranoid, is that a para with a nose problem? Even now, I can't help but joke.

I spot her standing in the window of our ten bed mansion. Higgins Hall as the press calls it. Better get it over. I could be broke by tonight and if she has her way, she'll put my trousers through the mangle, with me still in them.

In for a penny; I open the door with a flourish like Becks asking the Posh for a quick one.

"Yes, love. Thanks for your support."

Smooze her, let her see I care.

"You're a shit. Don't sit, you're not staying."

Her face makes thunder look like a sunny afternoon.

"I want to know how many accounts you got, and no lies."

Now, I'm still not sure that the game's up, otherwise she wouldn't ask, would she?

"One in Luxembourg and another in the Silly Isles. That's the honest truth, love," I say with open hands to show. "No lies."

"How much?"

Sara stands there, legs apart, arms folded, she means business.

"What?" I say eyes wide, like Rooney after a foul.

"Are you deaf and daft? You can screw as many young girls as you want. From now on that's your business. But don't try to pull one over on me, I want it all. Got it?"

"Yeah, yeah, okay. Should we say fifty-fifty?" I can't make it too easy.

"Bollocks. How about 100 nothing?" she spits out the words but there's that corbin glint in her eyes that would frighten my gran. I may be in the shit.

"I'll be broke. Come on, love."

"Don't 'come on love' me, Higgins, you should have thought about that when you couldn't keep your trousers on."

"75 25?" I ask, hopefully.

"All of it. Or I can go to the papers and they'll find out about the Arab princess."

That's out of order. If that comes out they'll never find my body.

"Ok, ok. Leave me a few quid to get by and the rest is yours, and the house."

Sara looks emolliated by that and walks over to the

39

desk, snatching a piece of paper and grabbing a pen, pointing it at me.

"Sign this, you piece of shit."

I'm hurt. There was no need for that. This is a momentous occasion. As big as signing a deal with Manchester United or being relegated.

So I sign, wasting no time. Before she can snatch the paper, I add a sentence above our signatures, 'In full and final settlement'. I get that stare, but what can she do?

Well, I'm off on my toes, out of that house as fast as I can. In my Jag, I make a phone call on my hands free. No mobiles whilst driving, I'm a good boy now.

"Willy, yeah, it's me. Still planning a trip to the Caymans?"

"Yeah. Wednesday? Book a seat for me will you?"

I increase the volume on my Bang & O and hum a tune.

***

Why is it always night when we fly to the Caymans? I watch the ground below getting smaller. I suppose it's a fine enough night for it though. The seat belt sign blinks out and the stewardess sidles along with a tray. About time too, this is First Class after all.

There're five glasses on the tray. No doubt four for me and one for the fat bloke in the next seat. He looks as if he was working on a building site before getting on the flight. What's he doing in First Class? Shouldn't be allowed. He's sleeping, almost purring.

"Champagne, sir?" the stewardess asks, offering the tray and giving me a tease down her blouse. I ease up to take a peek. That's what they're for, right?

"Delicious."

I grab a glass and down it in one then press my chest with the side of my fist and belch. The woman across the aisle leans forward and 'tuts' me. So I grab another glass and do the same with that, lovely stuff.

The bloke next to me is awake. He looks at me as if I've got two heads.

"You want to bag some of this, mate. Not bad, for plonk. I suppose you're not used to this stuff are you?"

He grins, showing a set of teeth that would have looked good on a camel. The stewardess leans over me and I get another eyeful. "Would you like a glass, sir?"

"No thank you, I don't drink. Could I have an orange juice, please?" says fat bloke.

I see my chance and grab it, 'he who dares wins'.

"Thanks, I'll take that then, love."

I thought she gave me the eye but it could have been indigestion; no taste these stewardesses. If you can't be a bit eager on First Class when can you?

I quaff the third glass and I'm as relaxed as Beckham on a testimonial.

"Do I recognise you?" I ask fat bloke, and offer him my side view smile.

Fat bloke shifts in his seat and I fear he might make the plane tip.

"No, I don't think so. I don't think we've met."

That's my opening.

"You recognise me though?" I ask. As if he wouldn't.

The stewardess comes back with his juice and serviette. The fat bloke takes it with a 'thank you', and sips like a girl.

"No I don't think so, should I?"

"Football?" I ask, looking at him as if he's light in the brains department.

"I never watch it and I've never played it."

He's taking the piss. Who hasn't heard of Rex Higgins? Liverpool and Manchester City? I'm speechless, almost.

"Well, it's bleedin' obvious you've never played mate. But I'm Rex Higgins?"

"Sorry, never heard of you. I'm Fred Mullins. Nice to meet you."

He offers his hand and his grip would do Vinny Jones

proud.

"What are you off to the Caymans for then, moody bank account?" I laugh at my joke.

"No, HMRC," he says with a grin.

"HMRC, What's that then?"

Then I remember, from my tax guy. Oh bloody hell. Think quick, Rex.

"Her Majesty's Revenue and Customs investigates fraud and hidden money? You said you're a footballer?"

"Yeah, I'm out there to play. I'm knackered mate. Mind if I sleep?" I say, perhaps a bit too quick.

"Be my guest. Me too, but if you want to talk bank accounts, wake me. Alright?" he offers.

I didn't answer and gulped the last of my bolly.

***

Out of the window I see we're circling Owen Roberts International Airport on Grand Cayman. That's at least twice the pilot's been around. I hope we're not going to crash land. I didn't come all this way to collect my dosh, to find myself dead on the runway. The stewardess is here again with champers. About time. I see the fat bloke from HMRC is waking. My luck to be sitting next to a fat bastard from the HMRC.

"Awake then I see," the fat bloke says.

"So, this investigation in the Caymans then."

"Who said anything about an investigation?" he asks with a cheeky grin.

"Yeah but you are, aren't you? So, what you investigating, secret accounts?" I ask.

"Why would I be doing that? You worried or something?" he asks.

"No. Not me. Clean as a whistle me. Anyway, everyone does it."

"Do they? We'll be arriving in the Grand Cayman soon. It's always best if you come clean early."

What's that supposed to mean? Does he know, or has the wife fingered me?

"Why would I come clean? I ain't got nothing to hide," I say.

"I never said you had. But if you did, then it would be easier on you if you told me before we land," he says it like a policeman, and squints at me.

Bloody hell, he does know. I'll swing for that cow when I get home.

"Okay, you got me. What you want to know?"

"How much, which bank and for how long?"

"Ten mil, Cayman Central, five years. Ok?" I say, pleading.

I'm relieved, a weight off my mind.

"That's better," he says, patting my arm. "I was joking. I'm an archaeologist, not with the HMRC."

Fat bloke's grin says 'cat's got the cream'.

8
MAYDAY
By Vesla Small

As Erling boarded the speedboat ferry, relief came over him. The decision to leave everything behind had taken time and had been difficult. He took one last puff from the hand rolled cigarette before throwing it on the ground and standing on it. Erling had rolled the same brand tobacco since his early teens, and his tarred, nicotine stained fingers were evidence to this indulgence. This would be his last cigarette.

As the boat glided past islands and reefs, the fresh sea air blew on his face. With the seagulls screaming and swooping behind the boat, Erling felt closer to the fishermen's and birdwatchers' paradise. The thought of it brought an extra beat of happiness to his heart.

Erling had read about the depopulation on the Island, with only ten permanent residents, which appealed to him. He preferred his own company rather than that of other people, and looked forward to peace, at last. But harmony was not the only thing Erling sought. He was forty one and was trying to prepare the way for a better future. People considered him emotionally inhibited, and people had called him many names, 'odd ball', 'spitfire' and 'angry young man'. He reflected on his ill reputation and agreed he was headstrong and at times he could be difficult.

After the factory closed, where he'd been employed all his working life, he'd been made redundant, almost two years ago. The last year had been financially difficult and demoralising. When his long-time girlfriend had left him for a woman, it had been a humiliating and shocking experience for him. What else, other than dislike, could be expected after this, he wondered.

Being diagnosed with 'chronic asthma' was the final blow. It made him bitter but above all scared. The work in the factory had taken its toll, added to that, his smoking. After a few serious asthma attacks, followed by hospitalisation, he'd decided that he needed a radical change in his life. His doctor had recommended a healthier life style and clean sea air. So, here he was, on board the speedboat, on his way to the Island.

The sea wind was brisk, and Erling huddled inside his windproof anorak. He sought shelter from the weather inside the cafeteria, where he could quench his thirst with a mug of coffee.

An odd group of people caught his attention. A foreign looking woman accompanied two young children. The youngest, the girl looked cheeky and seemed wilful, whilst the eldest, the boy smiled, and looked submissive. What struck Erling was that neither of the children were the same race as the woman. Erling balanced the tray with coffee and cake and sat at the same table as them.

"I'm from Sierra Leone. My name is Lucee," the woman said. "These are my stepchildren, Ola and Kari."

She appeared too forthcoming and talkative for Erling's taste, so he nodded as he sipped his coffee. Nothing else was said until the little boy interrupted the silence.

"Why are you sad?" His innocent eyes stared at Erling.

Erling felt uneasy at such a question, and looked at

the boy with surprise, unaware he'd made such an impression. But he didn't respond, instead he looked out at the sea, to avoid the boy's eyes.

"Did someone die?" the boy sounded concerned.

"No, I'm just tired," Erling responded.

"Their father died in a car accident last year," the woman apologised, put her arms around the boy, and kissed him on his forehead.

Erling raised his eyebrows, and mumbled, "It happens."

The woman grimaced. She looked at Erling, and busied herself with the children.

It wasn't that Erling didn't like children, he wasn't used to them. He had been an only child, brought up on a farm and rarely associated with other children after school. On the farm, it was work, work, work, and no time to play.

It crossed his mind he ought to make an effort, so he asked the woman, "Are you visiting friends on the Island?"

"No, we're moving to the Island. I'm a primary school teacher."

Lucee explained that after reading an article in a newspaper, inviting 'outsiders' to repopulate the Island, they'd decided to give it a try.

"But there're only ten people living on this Island," commented Erling.

"Yes, that's right, and now there'll be thirteen. And during the summer months, the Island will buzz with tourists," she laughed, showing a row of perfect teeth.

Her laughter was contagious, and Erling returned it with a shy smile.

"There are many summer houses on the Island, but they're old and cold and not suited for living in the winter," Erling sounded kinder. "I know from experience."

"We come prepared," Lucee laughed.

Erling found her friendly and easy going, and there was something about her, revealing a strong woman who didn't give up easily. She gave him the impression to be someone who'd been used to making an all-out effort, someone who'd experienced hardship. He was taken by her laughter and her smiling eyes. Despite her broad snub nose and a repaired harelip, she wasn't entirely unattractive. The jeans and the red pullover showed a slender and athletic body. Although curious to hear more about her plans, he didn't ask further questions, aware that they would stay on the same Island for the foreseeable future.

When the speedboat arrived in port, Erling spotted Per and his wife, Marit. Ever since Erling's visit to the Island, a few years before, they'd kept in touch. After Per had a heart attack, he'd contacted Erling, and had asked him to help with his fishing that winter. They'd agreed to lodge Erling for the next few months.

To his surprise, Erling was pleased to have met Lucee and her children, and was happier with his decision to stay on the Island. After he'd said goodbye to them, he saw that an old couple came to pick them up.

"Petter and Lotte are helping Lucee and the kids to settle on the Island," said Marit, as they walked away. "They live on the other side of the bay."

Hearing a dog bark, Erling bent and patted Rask's head. It was the same setter, the longhaired bird dog they'd had when Erling visited the Island last time.

As they walked up the hill, Erling saw the red painted timber house. The bleak sun shone over the slates covering its steep roof, and the chimney puffed smoke. Erling saw that nothing had changed and was pleased to be back.

As they entered the house through the narrow hallway, he smelt Marit's homemade meatballs in brown sauce. They sat around the kitchen table, with a view over the sea. Erling was hungry, gulped the food and accepted seconds. They talked and listened to the radio, the heat from the wood-fire made him heavy-eyed and sleepy, the sort that dreams are made of.

***

He was on the fishing vessel. The plentiful catch of cod and the one hundred kilogram halibut were more than they could hope for and weighed the boat down. 'Viking', an equipped fishing vessel, was on its way back to the port after a day's fishing. The fishing boat lay heavy in the sea. The fishermen drank coffee in the Captain's cabin and watched the waves increase in volume. Erling knew that Per was an experienced Captain who always ensured the safety of his crew at sea, but this time he was caught out. The gale arrived earlier than foreseen, and the waves increased to 14-20 feet, with the vessel rocking and rolling in the sea. The fishermen regretted they hadn't sought refuge before the onset of the gale.

"Mayday, Mayday, Mayday. This is fishing vessel 'Viking'. My position is, 65°19'33North and 7°19'3East, outside Halten lighthouse. Mayday. 'Viking' has a crew of five, and needs help. Mayday, Mayday, Mayday."

Erling could only just hear the Captain's message, with the storm raging outside. He rushed to the deck and drew up short.

There was no response from the Coast Guard to the Captain's distress signal.

The dark waves whipped the fishing vessel's sides while the crewmembers gathered on deck. Erling felt the deck leaning when the cargo of fish moved. The men pushed their way forward to the lifeboat, fearing that the ship would capsize. Four of them climbed on board the raft, but Erling was not quick enough.

With his hands clutching the deck's railing, the icy black water engulfed him. Weak and cold, he saw a woman inside the cabin house. Was it a hallucination, due to tiredness and loss of concentration, he wondered. Although he couldn't see her face, he knew it was Lucee.

With the crew and the lifeboat gone, he was the only person there to save her,

At last, he released the lifebuoy, moving hand over hand along the deck's rail. Exhausted, he snaked his way forward along the deck, grasped hold of the cabin door, and pulled it open. She was there. With the lifebuoy over Lucee's head, he tied a lifeline between them, and with his arms around her body, he plunged into the freezing water.

At first, he felt the water pushing down on them from all sides. The icy water and the darkness engulfed them. Despite exhaustion, he continued to struggle his way up, until he saw lights through the water and heard the noise from an engine above their heads.

***

Erling woke with a start as a hand shook him,

"Come on Erling. Get a grip. We've invited Lucee and her kids across for coffee and cake. She'll be here in a minute. You look dreadful."

His hand brushed across his face as he tried to wipe away freezing water, only to find four day old stubble.

9
EVERYDAY LIFE
By Jake Corey

Barry didn't understand why he was standing on the roof. He tried to move, to step back to grasp the railing but failed. Something stopped him moving, even his eyelids. There was no sound when he shouted. He willed his muscles to obey, they wouldn't. Fear gripped him. Something urged him to stop resisting. Barry looked straight ahead, over the London skyline but he couldn't turn his head. Despite the murky London air, in the distance, he saw the OXO Tower and to the right the twenty-three story Union Jack Club. Even further over, the Vauxhall building stood as a fortress. The River Thames meandered, indifferent to his plight. A movement behind him caught his attention but he didn't react.

'It will be alright, you only have to 'relax' and accept the inevitable. Fall forward.'

Where had that come from? There was silence, he was alone. The sensation inside his head was far more seductive than any siren.

'Accept and I'll release you. Ok?' said the thing in his head.

'Ok,' thought Barry. At least if he could move, he

might either escape his tormenter and jump off the roof or step back. This might have been a nightmare except it was real. What did he have to do to 'accept'? The inevitable he supposed. But if it was inevitable then he didn't have to accept it.

It had released him, he could move. That was easy. He stepped back and grasped the rail behind him. Barry sucked in air as if a giant hand had stopped pressing on his chest.

He looked into the street, fifteen stories below and saw the women's faces. Their features were unclear, the same as the other times he'd been in this quandary. It was like the London smog. Barry lived on the fifth floor but he often came here to be alone, to get away from people and from himself. Here Barry was whoever he wanted to be.

They always wanted something from him and he dared to contemplate what it might be. He remembered now. They wanted him to jump to his death. The women shouted to him.

"End it. Jump Now!" they chanted. "End it. Jump Now!"

It was no use. It penetrated his brain, reverberated, getting deeper, more intense.

"End it. Jump Now!"

"Jump! Barry, jump!"

His face itched and he touched a spot on his cheek, one of many. He picked off the scab with a nail.

Amid their incantation, a lone female voice shouted above the other demanding, "What are you waiting for?"

He hated himself and he hated his life, he hated this body that trapped him.

'There's no point in continuing, on holding out. It won't get any easier. We have a deal, remember? Accept,' the disembodied voice said. It reminded him again, he was useless and inadequate compared to the rest of the human race.

"End it. Jump Now!" they yelled.

Their upturned hands implored him, welcomed him, offered to catch him. It would be so easy, so quick, so final. Then his troubles would be over. An end to the chanting, an end to his torment, forever. It made such delicious sense.

Barry decided and stepped right to the edge, his toes an inch over the edge. His decision made, calm descended on him. Even his spots had stopped itching. There'd be no more taunts, no more comments about him being boring, smelly. No more sleepless, sweaty nights fretting whether anyone in the world liked him or even cared for him. 'End it now', he heard in his head.

The instant he decided, the chanting stopped. Silence, except for the sound of a slight breeze. A coolness on his cheek, a velvet covered hand stroked his face. Even the breeze tried to coax him into taking his final step, leading to his ultimate release. It made sense. Not only to the hundreds of faceless women down there, but to the wind, so it should be obvious to him.

One final step, lean forward and then … nothing. The upturned arms of the women were ready to welcome him. Why did he hesitate? A queasiness in his stomach, and his head filled him with dread. But this would be so…final.

"Get on with it. I have to get to work," a woman taunted. "You're a bloody coward. Let's see you jump, Barry."

They even knew his name.

"If you're going to jump, jump," a woman shouted.

"Don't keep us waiting. I can't wait here all day. Jump, you spotty snotspot."

They laughed at him, and thought him a coward for not jumping. Well, he was as frightened as hell. But to be thought of as being a coward frightened him even more. That he couldn't bear. He may be spotty and malodorous, he may have a problem with, well, he had to admit it, at least to himself, with girls, but he was no coward. This would end, if he accepted his fate.

SIGNPOSTS

He edged forward and leaned into mid-air. Relax, he had to relax, let go of the railing then blessed relief. So wonderful, so welcoming and a final proof of his bravery.

Fingers slipped on the wet railing. Even the railing conspired against him, begging him to leave it behind and fall forwards to embrace the women. He simply had to fall into their upturned arms and prove his bravery.

Now he was calm, relaxed and happy, now that he'd chosen. Relieved, his fingers slipped from the final anchor and he fell forward, falling, falling. His mouth fell open, trying to scream but there was silence. The wind sounded seductive and offered to enfold him. The women's laughter and the banging persisted. Something or someone insisted in breaking into his calm, into his moment of bravery, into his transport of delight.

The shouting was replaced by a banging accompanied by the theme tune to 'Batman'. He was in his own bed. Relief flooded over him, but he knew that last night he'd had the same dream he'd had every night for as long as he remembered. Was it chance or had he deserved this ride into madness? With a start, he sat bold upright. Icy breath caught in his chest and sweat ran the length of his back. He realised it must be Cubic, banging on his flat door.

"Jesus," gasped Barry, rubbing his face.

"Barry, get your idle arse into gear and get yourself out of that bed. Now!" Cubic shouted in her Welsh brogue through the door.

"Come on Barry, you'll be late for work. Get a grip," she insisted.

He wiped his hands across his face and looked at the wind up Batman alarm clock. It read two 'o clock. Surprise shot across Barry's face. He threw back the covers and padded across to open the door for Cubic and to face the flak.

Cubic blocked the doorway with her bulk and pointed a finger at his chest. She looked more frustrated than angry. "You're late again. Get dressed and brush your teeth."

Cubic showed no surprise at the sight of Barry wearing only his grey boxers and a Superman T shirt. And Barry showed no surprise at her abruptness, Cubic didn't want air in her conversation.

"Can you phone for me? Please?" pleaded Barry.

"This is the last time I'll cover for you. I'll tell them the electric went off and your alarm failed. Now move it. I made you a sandwich. Cheese. Eat on the way to work."

As Barry went to shower and cleaned his teeth, Cubic made the call. How could he manage without her? She bullied him, got him ready for work, kept him clean, more or less, listened to his sad stories and laughed at his Superman jokes. She even occasionally made food for him and acted as his protector and gobmonster.

"This is Barry's friend. Thanks, I'll wait."

Her voice sounded over the noise of the cascading water.

"Thanks. Barry had a problem last night. The electricity went out in the whole block and his alarm didn't go off," said Cubic in a business-like way, but loud enough to wake even the deaf Mrs Jones on the top floor.

Barry came out of the bathroom, dressing and brushing his teeth at the same time. As he pulled on his grey shirt, Cubic put a hand on an ample hip, holding the phone to her ear.

"Listen, Mr Smith, if I say the electric went off, it went off. Right? I'm not lying," she said in a firm, no nonsense voice.

A good excuse, a quick thinker. Now the government had brought in fuel rationing, there was no telling when the power would be on. Most of the power was reserved for essential services, such as government buildings, the military, trains and government ministers' limousines. Even fuel for planes was limited to military plane and government travel.

"He'll be in as soon as he can," she continued. "And don't you give him a hard time either."

The phone clicked off and she looked round at Barry, still stuffing his shirt into his trousers, as he reached for a jumper. She even lied for him.

'Thanks for short, round, hippo like angels,' he smiled, zipping his trousers.

"Smith says he's got something important for you to do today and he wants you to wear a jacket. Wear the brown one. Oh, and a tie. Here, take this," she said, stuffing a tie into his hand.

Twenty minutes after Cubic's banging and his feet touched the threadbare carpet, Cubic slipped a 1953 edition of a 'Flash Gordon' comic into his bag, handed him the bag and pushed him onto the concrete landing.

Barry normally took the stairs but he felt half-asleep and headed towards the lift. Whether it worked was a different matter. As he arrived, the lift approached the fifth floor, a good sign. As the lift doors opened the overpowering stench of bodily fluids almost made Barry change his mind. Fortunately, he hadn't had his breakfast and decided to risk the short trip. He took a deep breath, entered the lift and pressed 'Ground Floor'.

As Barry idly read the graffiti he learned that 'Luke Loved Lucy'. Regardless, Luke didn't have a career as a poet. Luke had also written, 'Luke gave Lucy a kiss then went in the corner and had a piss'.

It dawned on Barry that because he was standing in the corner of the lift, his shoes would probably smell of Luke's micturition. As his eyes moved on to the next piece of literary wisdom, he realised that the lift was rising rather than going down to the ground floor. The lights indicated that he was approaching the tenth floor. Barry stabbed the Ground Floor button and let out his breath, which he realised he'd been holding.

He'd sensed it would be a bad day when he slept in, now he knew. He should have walked down, it would have taken half the time. Seems he would have to walk from the top. Mr Smith would be furious.

As the lift doors slid open, Barry saw that the lift had gone past the top floor and stopped at the roof. A freezing bayonet slid down his spine as he stepped out of the lift and walked into the sunshine, as he'd done so many times before.

Barry was not a volunteer and this surpassed coercion. Coercion implied that he had a choice, but he had none. He imagined that this is what a passenger would feel like in a car going over a cliff. Whilst his brain screamed, his body wept with icy sweat. Knowing that he was still in the nightmare made it harder. He was at the mercy of his own imagination and only he knew its depth. His shoulders sagged and his legs started the plod to the edge of the roof. Even before he reached that point, he heard their incantation.

"End it. Jump now, Barry!"

10
MOMMY CLOWN
By Vesla Small

"It's the hospital. Elias's condition is worse, and he's asking for you," the nurse sounded worried.

Hanna was leaving her apartment to meet friends for a Chinese meal in town when the phone rang. She rushed down the stairs of the apartment building, and almost bumped into Jacob, her Jewish neighbour.

"How's it, lass?" he asked, and smiled at her with his lovely, soothing smile that usually brightened up her day, but not today.

"Not good, I'm afraid," she answered, sounding sad.

She rushed to her car, dropped into the driver's seat and turned the ignition key. The car didn't start at once, and she panicked. Finally, she heard the engine run, after she'd stamped on the accelerator and turned the ignition key several times.

'What a relief,' she sighed.

She called her friend on her hands free cell phone, warned her she wouldn't be able to make it to the restaurant.

On her way to the hospital, Hanna's thoughts went to Elias and how they'd become so attached to one another.

Hanna had entertained ill children for the last ten years. As long as she could recall, she'd been an able entertainer and good at 'clowning'. When her daughter was diagnosed with leukaemia, with frequent hospitalisations and treatments, she realised how her acting distracted children from pain, fear and isolation. So, when her Emma, at the age of five had died, she volunteered at the hospital as 'Mommy Clown', during her spare time.

Hanna had experienced both pleasure and sorrow during the time she'd performed for the children. The healing and soothing effect of her 'clowning' was not only for the benefit of the patients' mind, but also hers. After Hanna's husband had died in a car accident, some years after Emma's death, her life would have become intolerable, if she hadn't found the courage to continue her visits to the little ones.

Although she was every little patient's Mommy Clown, she often had a favourite. At that time, she had bonded with a little boy called Elias who, like her daughter, suffered from leukaemia.

Her affection for Elias had become special and strong, and she loved him dearly. Maybe this special friendship was because Elias's parents were drug addicts, or was it something in Elias that reminded her of Emma? Just like Emma, Elias was so pure and innocent, funny and happy, inquisitive and sensitive.

To give him a needed break from the hospital and its environment, Hanna had on occasion, taken him home to give him the feeling of being with a family.

On this particular day, Elias's health had taken a turn for the worse and the nurse who asked her to come to his sickbed, had told her he'd whispered, "I want my Mommy Clown."

Emma thought to herself, as she rushed through the hospital corridors, 'This is not the time for clowning. It's the moment to hold him in my arms, to make him comfortable and loved.'

Tears ran down her cheeks, as she begged for mercy, "Please help him, God!"

When she entered the Emergency Room, Elias's lips curled into a faint smile. He held out his arms and whispered, "Hold me tight, Mommy Clown. Hold me..."

While she embraced him in her arms, he took his last breath.

'My little Emma would have been fifteen years old,' she thought, her cheeks wet with tears.

Hanna prayed that she would gain strength to continue her commitment as Mommy Clown.

When she arrived home late that evening, she met her neighbour, Jacob, standing in the corridor outside their apartments.

"Come inside, into the warmth, my dear. I'll prepare you a nice cup of tea," he said in a quiet voice, and placed his arm on her shoulder.

A wave of emotions came over Hanna. She burst into tears, and between the sobs, she said, "Elias is gone... They couldn't save the little lad."

Jacob stroked Hanna's hair and held his arms around her, "Hanna, I've never told you about my life and my struggles. This is now the right moment."

"Before the war, I had everything a man could wish for. I had a promising career, money, property, a wonderful family and good friends. I wanted nothing more," he took out a handkerchief and blew his nose. "As you know, during the imprisonment in the concentration camp, the Jews' lives were doomed. The chamber of horrors, where my beloved wife and my darling daughter, six years of age, were reduced to ashes, is still fresh in my mind."

Hanna saw that Jacob could no longer hold back. One moment, he sounded happy and the next angry. His facial expression changed from joy to horror. Hanna had never seen Jacob that way.

"After the horrors of concentration camp, came the

difficulties of healing. I had nobody to turn to, no one to comfort me, only myself to rely on."

Jacob took a sip of tea, and looked at Hanna, "I didn't get where I'm today without working hard. My struggles made me stronger, and a better man."

Hanna watched, tears streaming down Jacob's cheeks, and she took his hands in hers.

He looked at Hanna, and with a sad smile, he said, "Hanna, when a person goes through hardships and decides not to surrender, it makes that person stronger, so don't give up now. There'll be other children needing Mommy Clown."

Jacob placed the teacup on the table and picked up a tattered photo album.

"There, that's my wife, Gertrud and my daughter, Herma. Aren't they beautiful? I also have good memories of them and I treasure those."

Jacob smiled, closed the album and continued, "So, Hanna, let's look after each other and do the right thing by others."

11
SIMON
By Jake Corey

Simon was not a boy of habit. He was a boy of impulse. Not the buying sort of impulse, but action impulse. Like the time he jumped out of the bedroom window because he could and the time he brought 'JumpIt' a stray dog home because he was smiling at him. That was a disaster for him and for JumpIt. Simon's parents took JumpIt to the vet to be 'disposed of'. He was sad, very, very sad. Maybe someway, someday soon he'd see JumpIt again.

No, Simon was a boy of action, but also a dreamer. And often daydreams got him into trouble. Teachers were a continual source of amusement and food for dreams. For example, Mr Harper who taught English. To Simon, 'Harper' sounded like 'scarper', so he did, straight out of the classroom, along 'Down's Road', across the playing fields and along the canal. His parents weren't too happy that he'd spent the day with a 'tramp' as they called him, but Simon called him 'Smellum'. To him, he was almost the most amazing person ever. He'd been to 'The Ashmore and Cartier Islands' and they'd talked and laughed about Smellum's journeys.

When he'd told his parents, he said, 'I've spoken to someone who's been to 'The Ashmore and Cartier Islands'. He pronounced it very correctly and clearly, as if he'd spent a long time practising it, which he had.

Simon told them all about 'The Ashmore and Cartier Islands'.

"They're an external territory of Australia, consisting of two groups of small low-lying uninhabited tropical islands in the Indian Ocean, situated on the edge of the continental shelf north-west of Australia and south of the Indonesian island of Rote," Simon said, exactly as Smellum had told him.

His parents looked at him, open mouthed.

"They are one of the smallest territories in the world and have no permanent inhabitants," Simon said.

Not bad for a ten year old (and two days), although he had a knot tying certificate from the Pathfinders Club.

"Inhabitants' is a great word,' he thought. He'd use it to impress people. His parents asked him lots of questions about 'That Tramp'. Silly questions, but grownups seemed to ask silly questions. He refused to give in to their seriousness and giggled. His dad had poked a finger at him and said, "You pay attention to your Mum, young Simon, and answer the questions, or so help me if I don't tan your backside."

Grownups said such silly things. His mum went to the 'Tanning and Holiday Preparation Emporium'. She'd been tanned and now she was almost orange. So why would his dad 'tan his backside'? And why his backside and not the whole of it? That's grownups for you. Why did his dad want his 'backside' to be orange? They'd get over it, eventually.

As he walked along the road, he asked himself where television pictures were before they ended up in the television. That was a mystery. And why doesn't all water run downhill towards Australia and end up drowning the kangaroos, and is that how 'The Great Flood' started?

SIGNPOSTS

His mum had said, "Ask your dad," and then sighed. She blew out her cheeks and told him to eat his twiglets, which he was having for breakfast. His dad had said that tele pictures came out of 'The Aether'. Simon's dad had even spelt it out for him. Well he'd checked Google Maps and they didn't. There was no place called 'The Aether'.

The closest, according to Google maps, was Aether Street in Las Vegas, United States of America and that wasn't it, because it only had a population of two hundred and fifty and perhaps he'd go there one day to prove it. That meant dad didn't know. So, it was now his job to find out. As for water ending up in Australia, at this time, the question was pending. Or rather both questions, because there was also the less important question about 'The Great Flood'. That was also 'pending'. That was another good word, 'Pending'.

Simon kicked a stone but it didn't land where he wanted it, so he kicked it again. A car sounded its horn and he realised that he was walking in the middle of the road.

'Well, if stones land in the middle of the road, what more can you expect?' he thought. That should be obvious, even for a grownup. The road rushed up and swallowed up the car. Served it right.

He saw clouds in the distance and below them a place where roads met. Grownups called it the 'Four Lane Ends'. He considered that for a time, as the 'Four Lane Ends' came nearer to him, he concluded that grownups didn't know very much and didn't think very hard. Why couldn't they call it 'ThePlaceBelowTheClouds' or 'AfterTheChurchWithASpire', or 'BeforeAfter'? 'Cos that's what it was, 'Before After'. Because he reached it before he'd walk past it and then it would be after.

Anyway, here it was, 'BeforeAfter'. The labels on the four armed man said, 'To Mitherswaite' on one, 'To Town' on another, 'To Boggin' on third from first and 'ToNoWhere' on the last, which was also the first. That was a silly but good name and it made him laugh. He turned that way and went towards 'ToNoWhere', to see if there was anything or anyone in 'ToNoWhere'.

Perhaps he'd find interesting others there, the same as him. He was a little surprised to see JumpIt sitting at the side of the road towards 'ToNoWhere', waiting for him. JumpIt was smiling, but then again, JumpIt always smiled.

***

Simon wasn't surprised, but he was so pleased. He went over to JumpIt and gave him a huge hug around the neck. JumpIt rewarded Simon with a wash of Victoria Falls proportions, oh, and a smile.

JumpIt always walked on Simon's right, and that's where he walked now. To Simon that made sense, not only was he safer there from traffic but he was also Simon's 'Right Hand Friend', so to speak. That way he could lay his right hand on JumpIt's head and give him a twizzle.

He wondered how far 'ToNoWhere' was. Simon thought about that for a considerable time, at least a minute. He was excited and hankered after not getting there too soon. His dad always said that it was all about getting there swiftly. That's why he'd bought a 'BMY' car or whatever, he'd called it. Simon couldn't quite remember its name, but he almost did. Sitting in the back of dad's BMthingy, he saw why it was good to get the journey over quickly because it was soooo boring. This was different. This was 'his travel'. He'd call it his 'Great Travel'. That sounded big and important.

Simon felt the sun on his back and neck, and the wispy breeze ruffled the hairs on his neck. He'd taken his favourite blue jacket off, the one with 'Newcastle United Football Club' on a round badge on the front. He carried his coat over his shoulder, the way adults do. The breeze lifted the sleeve of his T shirt and whisked along his back. The warmth reminded him of the time at the beach when his mum had trickled sand onto his back as he lay on his front, pretending to be asleep. It'd tickled him and made him giggle, that was how his mum found out he wasn't asleep. She usually cheated. Then there was the time his dad had said that he should go into the water and be 'boyish' and go adventuring. He didn't know what 'boyish' meant and his dad couldn't explain it, and as far as he was concerned 'adventuring' is something called 'A verb' so he should have said '..be boyish and have an adventure', he didn't really understand how to do that.

JumpIt lifted his head as if he was looking at something in front of them and barked once, quite loud. Not an angry bark, more of a 'gruff' bark. Simon looked ahead to see if he could spot what JumpIt had barked at. There must be a reason, because JumpIt never made much noise, unless he had a good why for. Simon spotted JumpIt's tail wagging, rubbed behind his hairy, sticky up ears and twizzled him.

"Wotzit JumpIt? Wotzup?" he asked smiling, but Simon's eyebrows were squeezed together as if he was confused, but he wasn't really.

At that moment, there was a rustle at the side of the track. Now it was more a track than a road and a tiny grey bird fluttered out and landed on its back almost a yard in front of Simon. The little tweeter shook itself before getting up on its unsteady feet and stood facing JumpIt and Simon. It tweeted once, he was sure it was a question because the tweet turned up at the end. Simon smiled but was concerned. The tweeter looked as if he might be poorly. JumpIt barked again, once. Not a warning bark, but a 'Hello' bark and his front paws left the ground as he did it. They always did.

"Hello tweeter. Are you hurt?" asked Simon.

"Tweeter my name not and not hurt I. Who might you be two? Coming here a wandering all place over and break quiet and come trouble cause to, I'll bet. Well, right place for that come you," said the tweeter, ruffling its feathers and standing straight up.

JumpIt cocked his head to one side and did a small

'wuff' and smiled at tweeter. Simon twizzled JumpIt who looked up and smiled. JumpIt liked to think that he looked after Simon but to Simon, they looked after each other.

"What's your name then?" asked Simon.

"I not a name got but sure not 'tweeter'. I my own am I and I never gotted a name so."

"Why? Why did you not gotted a name?" Simon thought that he'd better use tweeter language. Tweeter looked small and youngish and he might not understand grownup.

"Thrown nest out was I. Early. Walk around now I try eat things that little is. What with him wrong?" asked tweeter looking towards JumpIt.

"Nothing wrong JumpIt with. We friends are," explained Simon. "Do you have friends?" he asked.

"No, explain I," said tweeter, slightly cross, and lifted his feathers. "I own am."

"Where do you live?" asked Simon.

"Bright not you," said tweeter. "I on own! Not someone with! Lone am!" Tweeter lowered his head and looked ever so sad. "Live bush in I. There," said tweeter and pointed with his beak.

Simon looked down at JumpIt and they both grinned. JumpIt gruffed again.

"Would you like to come with us, Tweeter?" asked Simon, smiling.

"Go where you?" asked the tweeter.

"To 'ToNoWhere'," said Simon, expecting more questions.

"Go a little I," he paused for a moment and added, "maybe."

"Jump up on JumpIt then," said Simon and realised that Tweeter didn't understand. "Jump you JumpIt back on," corrected Simon, getting the hang of tweeter speak.

JumpIt lay down but Tweeter looked insulted. "Fly I. Fly everso high I," said Tweeter. With that, he quickly flapped his wings, flew around for a minute, flapping wildly. JumpIt woofed loud in Tweeter's general direction and Tweeter landed on JumpIt's back, before almost falling off. JumpIt looked annoyed at the showoff.

"How long fly you?" Simon asked Tweeter.

"Long time. Much long time. All day try to learn now I," said Tweeter.

"Well I think, you're a great flier. But you must be careful," said Simon, knowing about these things. "Know you type of bird you?" asked Simon.

"Me no know no," said Tweeter from JumpIt's back as JumpIt got to his feet.

"I saw you in book birds of," said Simon.

Tweeter pecked at JumpIt's grey stands of hair on his back and pulled out a crawly thing.

"JumpIt jummy jumm," said Tweeter swallowing the morsel.

"You are a cuckoo, I think," said Simon.

"Yes?" asked Tweeter.

"Yes," confirmed Simon confidently.

"Yes? Cuckoo me?"

"Yes, Cuckoo you."

"Yes. Cuckoo me. Cuckoo me," tweeted Cuckoo excitedly, as he tried to hold on to JumpIt's back with his feet.

Simon had learned all about birds at school and cuckoos had two toes pointing forward and two pointing backwards. That meant that they could hang on tight to things like JumpIt's back.

'Easy,' thought Simon, congratulating himself. 'Zygodactyl', his teacher had called it. He spelt it out in his head, because he'd learnt it from his book of birds. Z Y G O D A C T Y L. Although it sounded like Tweeter might be a dinosaur, it meant that Tweeter was a Cuckoo.

"Come on, JumpIt and Cuckoo. Investigate must we," said Simon.

'Investigate' was a good word and he loved it; even more than 'Inhabitants' and 'Pending'. Cuckoo and JumpIt looked confused, but they also looked happy.

"Cuckoo me, Cuckoo me. Cuckoo I friends with," said Cuckoo, trying to jump up and down to the annoyance of JumpIt who made a gruff, but in a friendly way.

"Yep, Tweeter's feet are for sure, Cuckoo."

Simon smiled at his two friends, feeling the gentle breeze on his back as they dilly-dallied towards 'ToNoWhere'.

12
PREVENTION IS BETTER THAN CURE
By Linda Nash

They were quarrelling. What had started off as a discussion, as to where they should go on holiday, had developed, almost before they both realised, into an argument, and then into a bitter quarrel. Colin had suggested that they go to India for their annual holiday, but Maddy was less than enthusiastic. They had been to Kenya, the previous year, and afterwards she had vowed that she would never go on holiday again to a poor country. She had said this, as soon as Colin suggested India. He looked at her in disbelief.

"But you've never mentioned this before."

"I'm afraid that's not true. If you remember, when we returned from Kenya, I said that I felt sickened by the beggars and the terrible shanty towns surrounding the big cities. I said too, that I thought it was shameful that the tourists' money only lined pockets that didn't need lining, instead of going some way towards alleviating the terrible poverty in that country. I have also mentioned during the past year that I was tired of my job and needed to be doing something more worthwhile. You've obviously not been listening to me."

Maddy took a deep breath, trying to calm her rapidly beating heart. She disliked quarrels and hadn't intended that their discussion should go that far.

"Yes, I do listen and yes, I did hear you moaning about your job. But we all moan about our jobs, from time to time, don't we? I'm afraid I didn't take it all that seriously. Anyway, you don't honestly think do you, that the two of us deciding not to spend our annual holiday in such a country is going to make a difference?" She could hear the impatience in his voice and his usually pleasant expression had been replaced by a definite frown.

"No, of course not, but, as I have said before, I don't wish to see the beggars, the shanty towns and the grinding poverty, while you and I stay in a big hotel and spend our hard earned money, on whatever we wish."

"Where do you want to go then?"

Maddy was ready for his question, because she had spent a great deal of time thinking about it.

"I don't want to go abroad. I want to stay here in England."

Colin exploded, his dark eyes flashing. "You can't be serious. A big part of our reason for going abroad is the weather. It could rain for the whole three weeks. Where are you thinking of? Weymouth, Torquay or Blackpool?" he asked sarcastically.

Now it was her turn to be angry. She shook her head, pushing back her dark hair impatiently. "Give me credit for some sense. Anyway, it's not so much where I want to go, it's what I want to do with my time off. I want to do something worthwhile. After all, poverty and homelessness is a much larger part of this country than people realise, and I feel that I would like to do something to help."

"And what am I supposed to do while you are off do gooding?" he said angrily.

"You can either join me, or you can go on holiday on

your own, or with friends," Maddy said quietly, trying to defuse the angry atmosphere.

"If you think I'm going to spend my annual holiday, catering to the poor," he said. "After all, a great number of them are poor through not managing their money properly."

"That is so not true," said Maddy, trying not to lose her temper. "It's like saying that people go to food banks to see what they can get for free, whereas an authorisation is required. You and I are so fortunate. We've never known what it is to be short of money. We both had a secure childhood, with pretty well everything we wanted, to say nothing of a wonderful education. We left university and found good jobs immediately and in fact, I think it's true to say that we have never wanted for anything. Is it really so strange or unreasonable that I feel I want to give something back?"

"Oh, for heaven's sake, Maddy, what on earth do you think you are going to achieve in three weeks?"

"I don't know, but I would like to try to do something and see how it goes."

Colin looked at her in horror. "What are you trying to say? You mean that you're thinking beyond your three weeks' holiday. You're not considering leaving your job are you and doing volunteer work as a full time job?"

"Why not?" We decided some time ago that we weren't going to have children, so maybe I would like to do something more worthwhile with my life. After all, a couple only need so much money, don't they? If we'd had children, I would have left work to look after them."

"It's hardly the same," he said starting to sound resentful.

"I need to fulfil myself," said Maddy, trying to appear firmer than she felt. "I know it's a hackneyed phrase, but I want to help others less fortunate than myself."

"But Maddy," said Colin desperately, "why have you never said all this before?"

"I think I have, but you haven't been listening. The moaning about my job, as you call it, is part of it. It's something I've been thinking about for a long time and it's only now come together in my mind. I don't expect you to join in, but I would like you to support me in something I feel strongly about." She realised, as she voiced her thoughts, that she was putting their marriage to the test, probably for the first time in the ten years they had been together.

"I need time to think about this," he said abruptly. "I think you could have mentioned it before, instead of dropping this bombshell."

Maddy, wanting to stop the quarrel, went over to him and put her arms around him. "It's not really a bombshell, is it?" she said. "It's merely a change of direction." Of course, he was used to her agreeing with him, going along with pretty much all of his suggestions. It was clear he hadn't listened to her expressing her dissatisfaction with her working life. No wonder he was so upset, she had probably turned his world upside down.

"I'm going out for a drink," he said. "I need to think about what you have said and examine my own feelings on all of this." He picked up his jacket from the chair, grabbed his keys off the hook, then left the flat without saying goodbye.

Maddy stood there, wondering what to do next. Perhaps she should feel guilty for not having prepared Colin adequately concerning her feelings. "I don't see what more I could have done ," she told herself, "apart from giving in my notice. In any case, it's how I feel, and he is going to have to respect my feelings."

She went into the kitchen and continued preparing their supper, but when Colin did not appear, she ate hers, and put his in the oven to keep warm. Maddy then went into the sitting room in order to look at some information she had received from an organisation, which supported Food Banks while trying to combat poverty. They had written to her, offering her volunteer work at one of the centres they had set up for women and children, to see how she liked the work and perhaps more importantly, how she fitted in. The Charity had also told her, that in view of her background in administration, there was a possibility in the future for paid employment, should she wish it. She was saving this titbit for later, depending on Colin's final verdict.

It was nine o'clock before Colin returned home. Maddy was reading and waited for him to come into the sitting room and say hello. However, he didn't, but went into the kitchen, where she heard him open the oven and presumably get the plate out that she had kept warm for him. She sat there for a minute or two, trying to decide what she should do.

"I'm being silly," she told herself. "I've got to nip this in the bud, otherwise we'll end up not speaking to each other and then things could escalate." Maddy shuddered at the thought. She took off her reading glasses and with the forms in her hand went into the hall.

Maddy pushed open the kitchen door and Colin started in surprise.

"Sorry," she said, "I didn't mean to startle you." It was then she noticed that he had been crying. Maddy went over to him and put her arms around him.

"Darling," she said, "what on earth's wrong?"

"I didn't go to the pub," said Colin. "All I did was drive round and round, worrying about what you'd said. I had the strong feeling that what you were really saying was that it was not a change of direction in your job you were looking for, but you were tired of me and wanted out of our relationship."

Maddy was horrified. "Of course not. You saw something in my words that was simply not there. As I said before you went out, I want to do something worthwhile with my working life. I can quite understand if you don't feel the same, but would like to feel that I can count on your support."

He looked up at her, an expression of relief on his face and smiled shakily.

"Will you promise me something?" he said. "You won't become one of those typical do gooders, will you, you know, dirndl skirts, Jesus sandals, hair in a ponytail, an earnest expression and always preaching that what they are doing is the only way."

Maddy laughed. "I think you are confusing do gooders with hippies, but no, I promise, I won't."

"Of course you can count on my support, you have always been able to, haven't you? Let me finish my meal and then you can tell me exactly what it is you intend doing."

His meal finished, Colin poured them both a glass of white wine and Maddy explained to him what the organisation she favoured, had told her.

When she had finished talking, Colin spoke,

"I think it would be a good idea if you spend the three weeks on your own working in the Centre, getting a feel for what they do. After all, it will be completely different to what you are used to. I may go and see my parents, they could probably do with some help, especially since Dad has been rather incapacitated since his stroke. However, I don't rule out helping at a Food Bank, or anywhere else I could be of assistance, for that matter."

Maddy could think of nothing to say. She felt overwhelmed by his generosity, and she wondered for a moment whether their decision not to have children was a wise one. She realised at that moment what a wonderful father he could have been. But, she pushed this thought aside, that was after all 'water under the bridge.'

When she finally spoke, it was to thank him, but he brushed her thanks aside.

"Maddy, that's what marriage is all about, isn't it, supporting each other?"

She smiled at his earnest expression,, then said

thoughtfully, "Do you know, I find it unacceptable that there are so many people in our prosperous country that haven't enough to eat, and I do realise that what I intend to do is not going to make a huge difference, but sitting back and ignoring what's happening is not an option either. I realise, too, that it's not enough to feed people. That's only a temporary measure, but it's not the likes of you and I that can really change things. That's in the hands of the politicians. I think it was Archbishop Desmond Tutu who said something like, 'There comes a point when you need to stop pulling people out of the river. You need to go upstream and find out who is pushing them in.'"

13
JUST DO IT
By Vesla Small

"Thank you for coming. We can't understand what the prisoner says," the prison officer explained, as they walked along the corridor.

"He's dangerous," he warned her, looking into the prison cell, through the tiny window in the door.

Anna nodded, "Open the door, will you?"

This was not the first time the prison had called on Anna's services as a translator. Entering the prison cell, she looked around. The young man pounded his fists into the mattress, his lips pursed together. He glared at the unwelcome visitors. She felt sorry for him.

Confident she could control the situation, she turned to the prison officer, "You can leave now."

Anna and the prisoner watched each other for a while, before Anna walked towards him, "Hyvä Päivä."

"Hyvä Päivä," he sounded relieved.

His skinny face with wild eyes and the oversized prison uniform dwarfing his lanky body made him look pitiful.

She smiled, and reached out her hand to greet him, "Minun nimeni on Anna."

"Minun nimeni on Mikko," said the prisoner, grabbing

her outstretched hand with both his.

"Minun Mikko," he repeated and put his lips to the back of her hand.

Anna held his hand and suggested they sit on the bunk, the only piece of furniture in the tiny cell. The naked walls, the almost empty room and the small barred window, looked dismal. At first, Mikko moved away from her. They sat on the bunk for a while, neither of them speaking, until Anna offered him chocolate. He accepted it and savouring it, his lips curled into a smile. As they flipped through a magazine, making small talk, he loosened up.

Anna understood that the man had good reason for his aggressive behaviour. It was autumn, and the police had found him in a mountain hut where he'd sought shelter from the cold. He'd walked over the mountains and through the woods from Finland into Norway, trying to find work. Exhausted and famished, he hoped to find food inside the hut, but saw a bottle of Moonshine, which he drank. While he slept it off, the police caught him and when he became violent, they arrested him.

There was a knock on the door, and the prison officer reminded them that time was up.

"Please come back," he pleaded, a tear running down his cheeks.

Anna nodded, smiled and left the cell.

***

The prison called Anna to tell her that Mikko was depressed. He refused to eat and leave his cell. When she entered the cell, sunlight came through the window and shone over Mikko, reading a book. Mikko's face lit up when he saw the pile of books under her arm.

"Did you finish Aleksis Kivi's book, The Seven Brothers?" she asked.

"Yes, I did. 'Seitsemän veljestä' transports me into the past. I like the way Kivi describes the Finnish peasant, with respect, humour and...," he lowered his voice, "love."

Anna nodded, "Yes, I agree. I believe many Finns identify with the characters in The Seven Brothers."

"Did you know it was Kivi who wrote the first novel in Finnish? He makes me proud to be a Finn," he said, leaning back and flexing his fingers, a smile crossing his face.

Anna's parents had often talked about Kivi's epic novel, 'a classic amongst the Finnish classics'. Anna looked up and thought back to her childhood, sitting in front of the fire, during the winter months, her father reading to the family. She could still remember the poem by Kivi her father used to recite.

"To fall asleep in your embrace,
"Land of our dreams, what bliss,
"O you our cradle, you our grave,
"You the new hope we ever crave,
"Peninsula so beautiful,
"Finland for aye our all!"

Emotion overcame her, and Anna rubbed her eyes, to hide her tears. After she'd placed the pile of books on the table, she stood up, and said, "I'll be back soon."

"Anna, thanks for bringing the novel. That meant a lot," Mikko stood up, and gave her the book.

When Anna left the prison that night, she thought about their conversation. Mikko reminded her of the characters in 'The Seven Brothers', living alone in the wild, free of society's restrictions. She smiled to herself, pulled down the brim of her sou'wester, climbed on her bike and rode home.

***

One Saturday morning, when they drank coffee and ate cake in the cell, Anna discovered Mikko's unusual background and special talents.

"This reminds me of my childhood," Mikko sounded cheerful. "Every Sunday, our caravan smelt of cake."

Anna smiled when he held the cake under his nose to relish its smell.

"Caravan?" Anna was astonished.

"Yes, I grew up amongst acrobats, clowns and animals, in one of Finland's finest circuses," Mikko sounded animated. "Everyone that worked in that circus troupe became my family."

'That's incredible. Working in a circus,' Anna thought, and felt a series of questions coming. She'd known no one from the circus world and wanted to know more.

"My dream was to become a contortionist, similar to my parents," Mikko said. "My younger brother, Eero and I trained together, and we became performing partners."

Mikko told Anna of his life as a circus artist, and how he and Eero had gained fame in Finland for their performances as contortionists.

"We could twist into the most extraordinary positions. Our legs were as flexible as wet noodle."

Anna laughed with him. She enjoyed listening to his stories and couldn't get enough, and Mikko was more than willing to let her into his secrets.

There was a change in Mikko's mood when he explained how the amusement tax made the circus operations unprofitable and the circus had to close, in 1953.

"So, we lost our jobs," he sounded apologetic, and looked away.

Anna saw a tear run down his cheek, and said, "That's sad. What did you do then?"

"We continued to perform in domestic circuses. But sporadic jobs didn't stimulate the same way the old troupe did." He brushed his hand through his unruly hair, before he said, with sadness in his voice. "After Eero's fatal accident, I was heartbroken."

Anna was not surprised that with his brother and performing partner gone, Mikko had difficulty coping. His depression had resulted in him taking to drink.

"I disgraced my family," he muttered, looking at his hands.

Anna understood his grief, but he was young and had all the reasons for fighting to win, so she asked, "But you didn't stop there?"

"No. I always enjoyed drawing and painting scenes from the circus. It was the only life I knew, so when the trough was empty, I muddled through selling paintings, for a pittance," Mikko's voice wavered with emotions. "But when the sales stopped, I got involved in petty crime."

Anna listened to Mikko telling her about his life as a vagabond, and Toivo, his fellow drinker, who committed suicide. She had read about poor morale, due to shortage of work, with many people struggling to survive. Aware that the Finnish people were known for their willpower and tenacity, a rage built up inside Anna.

"What happened to your 'sisu', Mikko? Finns are famous for that."

"I lost it... for a while, being shameful of what I'd become. I cut off from my family and friends. I was feeling alone, and I continued to live rough until, one day, a local businessman bought one of my paintings, and offered to help."

"How?" she interrupted, and tried not to sound curious, and what Anna heard next was hard for her to believe.

The businessman and his wife had invited Mikko to live with them in their mansion, and they considered him as part of the family. Mikko concentrated on creating his art, and they helped Mikko putting together an art exhibition in one of the city's finest art galleries, where he'd sold several paintings.

"The 'Galleon' was my masterpiece. It's exhibited in the city's town hall," he sounded proud, his smile lit up the cell.

She was impressed to hear how he had worked the copper. He'd hammered it into thin sheets, and shaped them into a miniature galleon, including interior and exterior details. Even the sails were made of copper. 'It must have been a magnificent sight,' she thought.

"So, you became richer?" Anna asked.

Mikko looked away, reflective. "I lived it up, partying with other artists and celebrities, leading a wild life, with alcohol and drugs. I felt lost, with no sense of direction."

Mikko gave Anna the impression he could not solve his own problems. In the past, he admitted, he'd counted on other people to help him find a sense of meaning and understanding to his life.

"Back to the street, no money, no friends, it was inevitable," he mumbled, the despair in his eyes.

"That's sad, very sad," she said.

Anna sipped her coffee. When she asked Mikko if he'd met anyone later, prepared to help him break out of the vicious cycle, he answered, "I met a woman, twelve years my senior, and she was kind."

"Good for you," said Anna, realising that she'd spoken too soon.

"We were birds of a feather," he said, with a shifty look. "We became homeless and lived rough, surviving by stealing from others to get alcohol and drugs, until she died."

There was an awkward silence in the cell, broken by Mikko.

"I prefer older women," he laughed, and looked into Anna's eyes.

Anna sensed Mikko's affection for her and felt vulnerable. She'd volunteered to support him during a difficult time. A woman on her own, with him in a prison cell was wrong. Respect and distance were needed.

***

Anna didn't visit Mikko for a while. The prison officer told her later that he'd acted nervously and had often asked for her.

When Anna visited Mikko next time, her two children accompanied her. Plays, games and laughter replaced conversation, and Anna discovered a person full of play. Despite the language barrier between Mikko and the children, they could communicate, not so much with words, but with illustrations on paper. He produced a smaller 'Galleon' in his cell, not in copper but in wooden veneer, with sails made from the sleeves of his prison shirt.

***

Anna never had the chance to say goodbye to Mikko. Maybe he dreaded that moment.

Before the end of his sentence, when Anna and her children came to visit him, they learnt that he'd left. That morning, he'd escaped, the only prisoner to break out from that prison, through the bars of the prison cell's window.

***

Many years later, Anna received a letter from Mikko.

Dear Anna,

You'll be pleased to learn that I did it.

It will be my pleasure and honour to receive you as my guest during the inauguration of my art exhibition on Saturday the 27th of March 1967, in 'Kalevala Gallery', on 57th Street in New York.

You asked me once, what happened to my 'sisu'? Now, you know.

Thank you for everything, Anna.

Respectfully, Mikko

P.S. My wife, Aina, is also an artist. She's twelve years my junior.

14
THE STORM
By Jake Corey

As the air thickens and the light dims, anyone would think that it was night instead of eight o'clock in the morning. I stare out of my office window. The three-sided window with its iron, art-deco decoration frames the view into smaller areas. Like looking through a mesh at the world beyond. The view faces north, east and south. In the morning, the light beams in but not today.

The bushes outside, two metres to my right side partially obscure my view. This time of the year they have heavy, lip-shaped leafage. A yellow beak catches my eyes, a blackbird, an old friend, as it dives into the foliage for cover. No doubt it senses the oncoming storm. Even inside my concrete sanctum, I can smell the 'ozone' as we used to call it as children, and it brings mixed emotions. The coming storm is welcome. Nevertheless, it drags back memories of dread.

To the left and past the bushes six traffic lanes, extending from a few yards hither to about 100 yards thither. White slashes mark the lanes, some continuous, others broken, a few with arrows, some are lines. The traffic, as always, flows oblivious to my presence.

The grey road darkens to black as the heavens beat a dirge, marking an end of the world message on the six-lane battleground. A violent, purple, malevolent sky embraces us. Over there, the clouds are an impervious carpet of grey. A dark cummerbund encircles the whole arena, squeezing it. As the violescent light casts brightness and dark shadows across my landscape, the scene is set for a confrontation between the merciless heavens beating their beleaguered inferiors below into submission. The last ten years have told me that the road will survive for another day, though logic dictates that eventually, the rain will wear it down, like an old man worn down by the inevitability of his own demise.

Cars and an occasional truck slow to a pedestrian crawl as the downpour shows them equal indifference. The rain spits at them, bullets from a heavenly machine gun, attacking the people inside. There's a car I recognise, a stone's throw distant, the translucent rain contrasting against the black of the car. The raindrops beat the car; they splinter, bounce and join in a river, washing over it, cascading over the boot and onto the van behind. The van's windscreen wipers panic, almost shouting at the rain to stop this maddening onslaught. Barely in time it slides to a halt. These out of control beasts vie for space, each blaming the other for the rain hammering on the window, the slippery road, the threatening sky.

The bushes outside my window are supremely relaxed, taking the battering in their stride. Their leaves allowing the rivulet to cascade then scatter, protecting my little friend. Once in a while, a small branch taps on my office window. The wind was nothing more than a cooperative servant doing the bush's bidding. Tap, slap, smack, sclaff, and to remind me it's still there, every minute or so I hear a thwack, thump and thrash on the impenetrable glass.

In my little sanctuary, I, the omniscient observer, smile. But still, I'm humbled by this display. This is the beauty and menace of the sky's own orchestra, with supporting clouds, rain and streaks of light. The crescendo rises, swelling to a turgescence. Its display is boundless; blotched with crimsons, speckled with charcoal grey to the right. Over the houses, a dark patch fills a quarter of the sky, its blotched ultramarine, shines off the roofs. Over there, other roofs shining, stippled with their own hues of red and black.

And as I think that the show is almost over, that it's on the decrescent, a streak of white momentarily blinds me and halos the darkest cloud. I count, one hundred, two hundred, three hundred. CRASH as the sound reverberates around me, seeming to prove that I may be omniscient, but I am not omnipotent.

The van door flies open without hesitation. A leg appears and the foot steps into a puddle, impervious or perhaps indifferent to the cold and wet. It's fifty metres or so through the house to the side door and I open the gate and watch.

Across the six lanes, he stands in the deluge and stares in my direction. He squints and points at me. Water is already cascading down his Barbour jacket, but he seems not to notice. His hooded eyes are an umbrella for his face but in seconds, he's soaked.

His face would be enough to scare most, but as he stands square on, one arm hanging loose by his side, the other pointing, legs spread. Others might think that foreboding calls. A woman with a dog walks towards him. She hurries in the rain, expecting him to get out of her way. She curses. He's unmoving and unfazed. She passes unnoticed. He scowls, looking up to the sky. Has he suddenly noticed the downpour going on around him? He grabs a bag from the van and slams the door.

He leads with his stomach, but not overly so. It's more, lightly neglected fat than a lifetime of sloth but he carries muscle. But they pull at his frame. With mouth set, he looks like a man with whom one does not mess, at least physically. There's no doubt he has handled himself in the past and despite his sixty odd years, he might still be able to do so.

Regardless of the steady stream of cars crisscrossing in front of him, he walks across the road, looking straight ahead. His deliberate steps make temporary holes as he strides through the runnel running along the road. The rain doesn't even feature on his radar. I smile. He gets across the forty metres, looking neither left nor right. How does he do that?

As he approaches, his face widens. It looks as if it's been squashed from the top, his smile pushes out his ears. We've known each other for decades, but we still shake hands. It's a ritual. He has a big, rough paw compared to my smaller hand and his handshake is firm but I pull him in out of the rain. A smile breaks across his face but his lips remain closed. This is a modest 'Hey there', smile. Steve's not a man to overdo the conversation. He's conversationally economical and can't stand noise, or 'gibbering', as he calls it.

"Come in, you're soaked," I say jovially.

"No shit. Whose idea was this?" he asks.

"Yours," I say.

15
FORTUNE AND MISFORTUNE
By Vesla Small

Magda remembered the car accident, when her father had turned the corner in his Audi, skidded, and lost control of the car. She was sitting in the back with her twin sister, Catrina, whilst their mother was in the front passenger seat.

The sound of squealing tires, the exploding airbag and breaking glass still rang in her ears. The last thing Magda remembered, before she lost consciousness, was her mother's scream as the car hit the tree. When she surfaced, after a few days in a coma, she saw her father sitting beside her bed.

"Where's Catrina?" asked Magda.

Her father looked at her and reached for her hand.

"Catrina was badly hurt in the accident and she died, dear," he explained, with tears running down his cheeks. "It's very sad, and we'll miss her."

She cried in her father's arms until sleep overcame her.

The news left her heartbroken. Unable to express pleasure and sorrow, she cut herself off from everyone.

Magda often thought about the happy moments with Catrina, when they played in the woods, went fishing with their father, and sang with their mother. She treasured these memories but sadly, Catrina wasn't there to share them with her.

The loss of her twin sister, at the age of five, was devastating and the loneliness that followed was painful. Magda felt a mixture of grief and resentment. Recovery appeared to take an eternity. Would she ever get over her loss?

Her mother seemed worn out, and one day she told Magda and her father, she needed a break. Two years went by, and she hadn't returned. Magda continued mourning her twin. Before the accident, she had enjoyed life, but she changed and made no attempt to make friends.

***

Magda overheard her teacher, Sylvia Patterson speaking to her father, Frank Simpson.

"That child's gifted, Mister Simpson. She's got talent," said Sylvia, pulled her glasses down on her nose, looking up at Frank.

Frank cleared his throat, "What talent, Miss Patterson?"

"She'd rather tinkle away on the piano than play with the children at school. She's a different person when she hears music. Let her start music lessons," she suggested, buttoning up her coat, as she walked down the corridor.

"Sorry, but I don't have the means to pay for lessons, so it's out of the question," replied Frank.

"My musical background isn't bad, and I'll be happy to give Magda free piano lessons. She can practise at school. Let's at least try," Sylvia proposed.

Magda's heart skipped a beat, and she thought she'd love to have piano lessons with Miss Sylvia.

"She's got talent?" repeated Frank, and walked away, as if the conversation was over.

"But what if she has?" Sylvia interrupted and followed

him.

Magda saw that her father's mood had changed.

Frank looked at Sylvia, his eyes lit up, and said, "She'll not become another Mozart, but if it makes her happy, that's what counts."

"That's a 'yes' then," said Sylvia.

"Would you like to start lessons on Monday?" Sylvia asked Magda, smiling.

"Yes, please."

Magda skipped out into the schoolyard, sat on the swing, and pushed with her feet. She closed her eyes, and as her father pushed, her hair blew in the wind, the swing moving faster and higher.

Some days later, Magda watched her father make a piano keyboard out of cardboard and every day, she practised her finger positions on the homemade keyboard.

When Magda was nine, she was an able piano player, and a picture of health, but she still had no friends of her own age. The music, her teacher and her father were her world, making her happy.

***

As her father drove into the courtyard, the sign over the gateway read, 'Noah's Ark Rescue Centre'.

When they walked inside the enclosure, a dog came towards them. Magda patted her head, and the dog nuzzled up to her. The dog was anything but ordinary. Her coat looked like tangled dreadlocks, and Magda could barely see her snout. She felt straight away that the dog was special.

"I'll call you Scruffy," she said, and held a snack for the dog to eat.

"Is this the one?" asked her father,

Magda nodded, a big smile brightened up her freckled face. She attached the leash and walked towards the Reception Desk.

"She's abandoned. She's a gentle herding dog, and around three years old. She's micro chipped and spayed. Fifty pounds, please," said the keeper, almost out of breath in his desire to make a deal.

Scruffy became Magda's constant companion and confidant, and they enjoyed hours of fun playing in the forest.

***

One day, when Magda threw sticks for Scruffy, the dog disappeared into the forest. This had not happened before.

She heard the dog barking and walked in that direction. Scruffy stood near something lying on the ground. The thing moved, and it resembled a person.

"Who are you?" Magda asked.

There was no response, but when Magda walked closer, she discovered a boy lying under the old elm tree. She leaned down to get a better look. The boy's eyes were closed, and he groaned.

Because her father was at work, she couldn't ask him for help, so she left her dog to watch over the boy.

When Magda and Sylvia returned, they found the child with his arms around Scruffy's neck, looking cold and confused. He stared at them, brushed his floppy hair out of his eyes, and stood up.

"What's your name?" asked Sylvia.

"Lamar."

They could hardly hear him. Although he was conscious, he'd suffered from the effect of the fall, so they took Lamar to the school.

"Where do you live?" asked Sylvia.

"In the gypsy camp, over there," he answered, and pointed towards the woods.

Sylvia treated his cuts and bruises before they walked him back to the caravan site.

"Where's your school?" Magda wanted to know.

"I don't go to school," Lamar answered, and looked down.

It surprised Magda to hear that Lamar hadn't before been to school. Instead, his mother taught him in the evenings. During the day, he would help his father, who made a living as a metalworker.

"We don't mix with the non-gypsies. I play in the woods on my own," he explained.

'Just like me,' thought Magda, before she turned towards Sylvia, and asked, "Maybe Lamar can join my school?"

"Let's ask Lamar's parents first," suggested Sylvia.

When they arrived at the caravan, Lamar's parents were relieved to see them. They'd been searching for him in the forest. Pleased to meet the teacher from the local school, they accepted the offer for Lamar to go to Magda's school, and so began a lasting friendship.

Magda visited Lamar and his family often in their gypsy caravan. She enjoyed the atmosphere of the smoking fires in the gypsy camp, where she could listen to Lamar's father play the guitar, and his mother singing gypsy songs.

Lamar often stayed with Magda and her father in the red brick house near the river. Sometimes Frank took the two out fishing. And when Frank bought the old piano from the school, Magda could play the piano as often as she liked, with Lamar listening to her.

***

On this precise day, when Magda and Lamar walked through the school gate, Scruffy's barks welcomed them, as usual. The two friends patted the dog's head and ran down the road, with Scruffy at their heels.

Lamar spotted blue flashing lights from a fire engine, and shouted, "There's a fire down your lane!"

"Which house?" asked Magda.

"It's yours, Magda!"

She wanted to scream, but no sound came out. Something held her back, and no matter how hard she tried, she could neither move nor talk. Magda watched the blazing flames rise from what looked like her home.

Lamar grabbed her hand, dragged her along, and ran.

As the flames engulfed her home, she spotted an ambulance, and the paramedic carrying someone out of the house on a stretcher.

"It's daddy!" she cried through the crowd of prying spectators.

Too late, the driver closed the back door of the ambulance which drove off, its blue lights flashing. The sound of the ambulance sirens pierced her ears, and Magda covered her ears and sobbed. Just as fast, she ran after the ambulance, trying to catch up with it. Lamar ran after her and after a short distance, he stopped her, and she collapsed on the ground.

"Magda, there's nothing we can do."

Lamar's brows drew together, and he bit his bottom lip. Although, no more than ten, he acted like an adult.

Broken hearted, Magda felt her dog cuddle up against her, and whimper, as if to say, "He'll be alright."

Sylvia arrived, put her arms around her, and said, "Your dad's in the best of hands. We can visit him in hospital if you want."

Magda wept when she thought of her father and what might become of her,

"But before we visit your dad, we need to find a place for you to stay. I have a guest room, so maybe you'd like to stay with me for a while?" proposed Sylvia.

"What about Scruffy?" asked Magda.

"I've always wanted a 'watchdog' for the school, so she's also invited," Sylvia replied. "But, it'll be dark in an hour, so let's first walk Lamar home to his parents."

They walked along the forest path, past the old elm tree, where the children had met some months earlier. Lamar's parents greeted them when they reached the gypsy camp, and the smell of a 'hotpot' made their mouth water. Everybody sat around the table, and enjoyed the stew of meat and vegetables, in the homely atmosphere of their caravan.

***

A few days later, Magda and Sylvia sat in the car, on their way to the hospital.

"Magda, before we visit your dad, there's something you need to know," said Sylvia. "There're swellings and blisters on your dad's skin, so he doesn't look good right now. He's hurting, and they give him medicine to make him comfortable." She paused, took Magda's hand in hers, and smiled, "The nurses treated him quickly, so he'll recover."

Magda listened to her teacher and nodded.

After a while, Magda asked, "Are we there yet?"

"A couple of kilometres, but first we'll stop and buy flowers for your dad."

When they entered the hospital, they walked into a waiting room where they washed their hands and put on a hospital coat. Sylvia twisted her red hair into a ponytail to fit under the disposable hospital cap and then helped Magda to put on hers. Before they walked into the Burn Unit, they received slippers to put over their shoes.

Sylvia looked at Magda and smiled. "You look such a pretty nurse," she said, and pushed her gently into her father's sickroom.

Magda was anxious. She hadn't seen her father since that dreadful day.

"Thank you, Sylvia for bringing my little girl. I've missed her," said Frank, a tear ran down his cheek.

"It's my pleasure, Frank. She's as good as gold. We're both concerned about you," Sylvia replied.

When Magda came closer to her dad's bed, she saw he was smeared with ointment and covered in gauze. Her dad reminded her of the picture of the Egyptian mummy she'd seen in a book.

Standing on her toes, she placed a vase with the sunflowers they'd bought, on the top of the cabinet.

Her dad blew her a kiss, and said, "Thanks, Sweetie. They'll cheer me up when you're not here."

They talked about this and that, until a nurse came to give him the medicine, and they had to leave.

Magda was quiet on the way home, and Sylvia left her to her own thoughts.

When Sylvia put the child into bed and kissed her, Magda looked at her with tears in her eyes, and asked, "Dad will be alright, won't he?"

"We'll make sure he is."

When Sylvia kissed her again, Magda felt reassured.

***

Magda was playing in the schoolyard when Scruffy barked at the sound of the doorbell. An elderly man, dressed in a dark coat and hat with a brim, spoke to her teacher.

"I would like to speak with Magda Simpson," said the man.

Magda pricked her ears up when her name was mentioned.

"Who are you?" asked Sylvia, leaning over the gate.

"Philippe Piraux," he answered, with a French accent.

Magda stopped playing, when she heard her teacher saying, "Excuse me, but Frank Simpson has never mentioned any family, but please come in."

'Family?' wondered Magda and followed them. She watched them through the glass door while they drank tea and chatted.

Magda entered the room and stood in front of the white-haired man.

"Hello. I'm Magda. Who are you?"

Her innocent grin made the man smile.

"Magda, be prepared to meet someone special," said Sylvia. "This gentleman told me, he's your grandfather. His name is Philippe Piraux."

"So, I've got a grandfather," Magda said with wonder.

"Yes, Magda, I'm your grandfather. I live in Belgium, and I'm visiting you."

"That's nice," Magda spoke in a quiet voice, and turned away.

The emotions after her father's accident, and the news of a grandfather she'd never heard of were too much.

Philippe Piraux lowered his head, and said, "Magda, you're named after your grandmother, and she came from Russia. She would have loved to meet you."

The corners of the old man's eyes wrinkled when he smiled and touched her playfully.

Magda looked into her grandfather's eyes. She smiled, felt his white beard, and said, "Just like Father Christmas."

A tear ran down his cheek, and she dried it with the sleeve of her cardigan.

16
THE CLOCK
By Linda Nash

"Darling, you're sulking." Rosie's mother touched her daughter's arm gently.

"I know you loved that clock, but Granny didn't realise, and that's why she gave it to Kate for her birthday."

Rosie looked up at her mother, her blue eyes filled with tears and she angrily pushed her brown curly hair away from her face.

"It wouldn't be so bad, Mummy, if Kate wanted the clock. But do you know what she said, whatever did she give me that for? It's not fair, I've loved that clock for ever and ever."

"I know," said her mother. "But Kate would probably have said that about whatever Granny gave her. You know how she is. She only wants whatever is the latest gadget or fashion item." Her mother sighed, "It's all to do with being a teenager."

"I shall never be like that," retorted Rosie. She paused for a moment, thinking about the beautiful little carriage clock, with its painted enamel face and pretty, carved, carrying case. She had first noticed it when she was almost seven. It was sitting on Granny's dressing table, ticking away and chiming softly on the hour. Since then, whenever they visited their Granny, she would slip away to her Granny's bedroom and admire it, secretly hoping that one day it would be hers. She should have told Granny how much she loved it, then it would have been kept for her and Kate would have been given something else. Mummy was right, since Kate had turned 13 and officially become a teenager, she seemed to be a different person. They had always done things together, but now Rosie, had become the boring younger sister, who didn't understand anything. It was very puzzling and most hurtful, and the last straw was the clock.

Rosie sighed. She was only eleven, but sometimes it felt as though she was years older.

Grownups were always telling you that you were only a child and wouldn't understand, but they were wrong. You understood things perfectly, but had a different point of view to theirs. Of course, you couldn't say that to them, as you would probably be accused of being cheeky or rude. She sighed again, what was that expression of Daddy's, 'life was like a minefield'. It described her life accurately, as she found herself having to steer her way round her rather prickly sister and deal with her parents, her Granny, to say nothing of her teachers. She had to admit, though, she missed her sister's company and rather wished, in spite of what she had said to her mother, that she would soon become a teenager and be able to take part in Kate's life again.

Mummy was speaking again, "Daddy and I are very worried about Granny. As you know, she has not been well lately, and we are wondering whether she should come and live with us. After all, we have enough room. She could have the guest bedroom and as you and Kate no longer use the playroom, we could convert it into a sitting room for her."

Rosie looked at her mother in horror. It was one thing

going to visit Granny from time to time. She loved her dearly, but to have her to live with them permanently was something else. It was true, they didn't really use the playroom any more, but it was theirs and it was somewhere to put stuff.

"Couldn't you put her in a home," she suggested. "My friend Jenny's parents have put their Granny into a home. We could easily go and visit her there."

It was her mother's turn to look horrified. "Of course not. We have plenty of room here, and it would be much nicer for Granny to be with her family. She would probably be very unhappy in a home."

Rosie didn't get it. Homes were full of old people, weren't they? Her Granny was old and so it made perfect sense that she would be fine in a Home. She decided, however, that it was advisable not to say this to her mother. Thinking about it though, she realised that her Granny seemed to spend a lot of time resting and didn't join them on outings any more. Something occurred to her.

"Does Granny want to come and live with us?"

"Not really, but she realises she cannot live on her own any longer."

How strange, Rosie thought. You'd think that Granny wouldn't be able to think of anything nicer than coming to live with her family. After all, she was always so pleased to see them and seemed upset when they left.

Her mother looked at her watch and got up.

"It's time I prepared the supper. Would you lay the table, please?"

It was on the tip of her tongue to say that it was Kate's turn, as she, Rosie, had both laid and cleared the table, the previous evening, but seeing the worried look on her mother's face, she felt it better to simply lay the table and say nothing.

Later, as they were eating supper, her mother spoke again of having her grandmother live with them. Both

Rosie and her father said nothing, probably because they had already been told, but Kate, who always ate her meal without showing any emotion or saying anything, looked up and glared at her mother.

"You can't do that, and anyway where would you put her."

"She can have the spare bedroom and use the playroom as a sitting room," replied her mother.

"What?" said Kate. "That playroom is mine and Rosie's. Anyway, I shall want somewhere when my friends visit me."

'What about my friends,' thought Rosie, but wisely said nothing.

Her father intervened.

"The situation is difficult enough, Kate, without you adding to it. We will all have to be prepared to give up something, and anyway, most of the burden will fall on Mummy, so I expect you both to cooperate."

Kate leaped to her feet.

"Why can't she go into a Home?" she shouted. "All my friends' grandparents go into Homes."

Now, it was their father's turn to be angry.

"There is no question of your Grandmother going into a Home, while we have room here," he said firmly. "You had better go to your room and when you have calmed down, you will apologise to your mother."

Kate went red and silently did as she was told.

There was an uneasy silence following Kate's exit. To her horror and embarrassment, Rosie saw that her mother was crying.

"What are we going to do, John? We've got to pull together as a family to make this work."

John put his arm round his wife. "Don't worry love, there are bound to be teething troubles. Kate is being a typical teenager, her point of view being the only one that counts. She'll get used to the idea. You know how she loves your mother."

Rosie was not so sure about that. Kate always moaned to her about having to visit her grandmother and how boring she was. If she loved her, she was hiding it pretty well.

Her mother appeared to believe him anyway, as she smiled at his words and started serving the dessert. Mm, apple and pear crumble Rosie's favourite.

They had just finished eating, when the kitchen door opened and Kate appeared.

"Sorry Mum," she muttered, looking at her feet. "Your news was so unexpected."

"That's alright," said her mother, pushing a plate in front of her. "It's not easy for any of us, including Granny."

The next few weeks were very busy. Rosie's mother spent a lot of time at Granny's, having managed to persuade her that she should come and live with them. The girls had had to clear out their playroom. They had grumbled to each other, but had not dared to complain to their parents, as they knew their complaints would fall on deaf ears. Actually, it had not been too awful, as they had collected together their old toys, thrown away those that were broken and taken the remainder to a local children's home, where they were enthusiastically received. Even Kate seemed touched by the children's reaction.

"We're lucky, you know Rosie. They were so pleased that we gave them our old stuff. When you think that we have pretty much everything we want and it's always new."

Rosie looked at her sister, smiled and nodded. Her sister sounded more like the old Kate.

However, when they arrived home, there was a builder's van in the drive. Kate immediately started to complain.

"Oh no, I bet they're here to convert the playroom. They'll make so much noise. How shall I be able to hear my music and do my homework, with all that going on?"

Rosie was surprised. Kate listened to her music through

earphones, so she didn't see what difference builders would make, and as for her homework, she always seemed to have done it by the time she got home. She did seem to complain about everything.

She went into the kitchen, where her mother was making lunch.

"Oh darling," said her mother, "the builders have already started on the playroom. They said it would take about a week. How did you get on at the Home? I'm going to Granny's this afternoon. Would you like to come with me? I'm sure Granny would love to see you."

Rosie had planned to go swimming, but did not want to disappoint her mother.

"I'd love to, Mummy," she said, feeling guilty when she saw her mother's grateful expression.

On the way to her grandmother's, Rosie's mother chatted to her, mostly about how their lives would stay the same when her grandmother moved in with them. Rosie found this rather difficult to believe, but felt it best to keep quiet.

When they arrived at the house, they found Granny surrounded by jewellery. She smiled when she saw Rosie.

"Oh Rosie, how lovely to see you. Would you mind helping me to sort this out,

I want to keep the good jewellery and I will get rid of that which has little or no value."

"But Granny, I don't know the difference."

"That's alright, Rosie, you sit yourself down and I will show you what to do, but before we start, there is something I would like to show you." She pulled a pretty bracelet from one of the piles, which had little objects attached to it.

"This is made of silver, Rosie, and is called a charm bracelet. The little things hanging from the bracelet are called charms. The bracelet was the first gift your grandfather bought for me, and whenever he went somewhere without me, he bought a charm, which he attached to the bracelet. I know it's not your birthday yet, Rosie, but I wondered if you would like it."

Rosie hugged her grandmother. "Oh Granny, it's beautiful, are you sure?"

Her grandmother smiled and handed it to her. Rosie examined it closely.

Goodness, there was a miniature Eiffel tower, a tiny elephant, an aeroplane, even a little castle.

"Granny, it's lovely, will you tell me where Granddad bought the charms?"

Her grandmother laughed. "If I can remember, Rosie. That will be something we can do together when I move to your house."

Rosie spent a happy afternoon, sorting out her grandmother's jewellery. Some little pieces, which she liked and which she thought Kate might like, she took home with her.

When Kate arrived home that evening, Rosie showed her the pieces of jewellery she'd brought back with her. Kate, after glancing at them, turned up her nose.

"Ugh, they're awful," she said. Suddenly, she spotted the silver charm bracelet on Rosie's wrist. "Where did you get that, they're really cool?

On hearing that Granny gave it to her, Kate exploded.

"She should have given it to me, I'm the oldest."

"But, she gave you the little clock," protested Rosie.

"I'll swop you it for the bracelet. I know you love that clock and you were terribly upset when it was given to me."

Rosie could not believe her ears. Kate knew that she loved the clock and she had never said anything, she had even said that she didn't know why her grandmother had given it to her. Rosie was furious. She thought for a moment before she replied.

"No thanks, Kate. Granny wanted you to have the clock and me the bracelet. Yes, it's true I loved the clock, but it's yours now. I wouldn't want to hurt Granny's feelings, even though you couldn't care less, as long as you get what you want." She picked up the jewellery, smiled at her sister, who was looking at her open mouthed and left the room.

17
THE ALBATROSS
By Vesla Small

'What does it mean?' Sylvia wondered. 'I would jump at an interesting story for The Weekly Signpost.'

Her eye caught the outline of a cruise ship and a plane in the coffee grains, and at the bottom of the cup, she saw a vague outline of a triangular warning signpost.

The journal she and Manola had started six months earlier was promising at the time. Enthusiasm and commitment were always present.

'Where did it go wrong?' Sylvia thought. 'Maybe the readers are bored with the same humdrum stuff? Maybe we need to add a different angle? Perhaps a new co-writer or adventure is the answer?'

She was about to leave the café, when Manola appeared at her table, a bright smile on her face.

"Sorry I'm late. I bumped into Charlie. He's an offer we can't refuse. Let me explain," she sounded out of breath.

Manola could hardly sit still, crossing one leg, then the other, before she continued, "A media company based in New York is looking for two sharp and talented freelance journalists, like us... with physical endurance and alpine experience. They want us straight away, like tomorrow," Manola sounded overjoyed.

"No, no, Manola, this is going too fast. What about The Weekly Signpost? Who'll look after that?" Sylvia replied, level headed and calm, as usual.

Manola's eyes were shining with delight. "I long for something different to happen. We'll never get an opportunity like this again. Think about it. We'll join a growing and energetic team of writers and researchers. Our scientific education and your skills as photographer will be put to good use," Manola did her best to persuade Sylvia.

In Sylvia's opinion, Manola always seemed to take the lead, and was prepared to take risks. Concerned that Manola's thirst for change and excitement could end in disaster, Sylvia looked preoccupied, perhaps too long for Manola's taste.

"What's the verdict?" asked Manola.

"I guess we can do it, providing..."

"Providing what, Sylvia?" Manola sounded impatient.

"Providing Jack can look after The Weekly Signpost while we're away," Sylvia replied, unable to hold back a smile.

"I'm sure your brother will cover for us, so that's a deal," Manola winked at her, looking pleased.

Manola wrapped her arms around Sylvia, hugged her and then ordered wine to celebrate.

"To us!" Manola's eyes beamed.

Sylvia toasted her friend and noticed that Manola was too full of excitement to think of anything else.

There was little time for preparations and two days later, Sylvia and Manola were on board a United Airlines plane, on their way to Argentina. They enjoyed being waited on by the flight crew while they read and discussed the material provided by the 'FJEA', the Freelance Journalist Explorers Association.

***

"We're making the final approach to Buenos Aires Airport. Please fasten your seatbelts," a voice broke into their dreams.

Although their bodies felt stiff and sore after the long flight, they livened up when they saw the signpost 'FJEA', held by a man with a wide toothy grin, with an Argentinean look.

"Buenas Días Señoras. Welcome to Buenos Aires. My name is Juan-Way Santos. I'll accompany you to Caesar Park Hotel and show you around this beautiful city before your Antarctic adventures begin."

They enjoyed the prolonged excursion along the grand boulevards and the visit to the impressive palaces. But what left a lasting mark on the two women was when they stood on the balcony of the 'Pink House', from which Eva Perón had addressed the crowds of Perón supporters. The guide admired Eva Perón and spoke about the material contributions she'd left behind throughout Argentina. "She was the defender of the poor," he said, tears running down his cheeks.

Happy, overwhelmed and exhausted, Sylvia and Manola settled in the hotel room. Everything had happened in such a short time. The day reminded them more of a dream than reality.

***

The next morning, Sylvia lying in bed, yawned, stretched and smiled when she heard Manola's voice copying one of Madonna's songs from the film 'Evita', "What's new Buenos Aires... I'm just a little stuck on you. You'll be on me too..."

When they entered the reception, they found Juan-Way Santos waiting for them.

Although friendly, his voice sounded like a recorded

message, "The mini-bus will drive you to Pistarini Airport, outside Buenos Aires. A private charter will fly you to Ushuaia, the southernmost city in the world. Then embark the 'Antarctic Explorer' and set sail the following day. I enjoyed meeting you, but here our paths part. Hasta la vista!" He waved, pointed toward the vehicle waiting for them and left.

As the party boarded the charter plane, Sylvia reflected on the outline of the ship and the plane in her coffee cup three days earlier, and her heart did an extra beat.

'Was this really happening? Was this the dawn of a new vocation? Was this a new start for The Weekly Signpost?' These questions went through Sylvia's head.

The flight went smoothly until a gut wrenching explosion came from the tail of the plane. The plane jolted and there was a smell of burning machinery. People gasped and screamed.

The captain announced, "The plane has lost one engine. Everything will return to normal. In the meantime, please fasten your seatbelts and remain calm."

Sylvia felt the tension amongst the passengers, and grasped Manola's hand, holding it tight.

"Don't worry, the plane won't crash. The pilot has everything under control," her voice trembled while she comforted Manola, whose palms were bathed in sweat.

All of a sudden, the flight attendant told everyone to adopt the 'brace position' and to prepare for the worst. The noise and impact were incredible as they were thrown around.

Strapped into her seat, Sylvia was petrified when the plane hit the water. It bounced and skidded to a halt.

"Sylvia, we're going to die!" Manola sounded terrified, she gasped and closed her eyes.

"The plane's sinking. We're in the water. We've got to get out of here!" Sylvia screamed into Manola's ear, but her body seemed lifeless.

Sylvia pulled Manola over her shoulder and walked

towards the emergency exit, the waves lapping over the wing, as the airplane started to sink.

Submerged in water up to her waist, feeling the icy water, Sylvia pleaded, "Oh, God, please help us! Please don't let us drown!"

The freezing water embraced her body and pushed her further down into the darkness. She ran out of strength and let go of Manola's body while she felt the water engulf her. It was quiet, warm and full of light.

***

Sylvia heard voices around her and felt someone pulling her. When she opened her eyes, she spotted a fisherman, standing over her with a fishing gaff in his hand. At first, she felt frightened when she saw him stab the pole with its hook into her life vest, but then he carefully lifted her on board the fishing vessel.

An albatross followed the ship, flying high and gliding over the vessel.

"Hola!" he spoke in a quiet voice, wrapped a blanket around Sylvia, and carried her into the warm cabin, his eyes wrinkled as he smiled.

On the lifebuoy, Sylvia had seen the ship's name, 'Esperança'. She'd heard that an albatross following a ship was a sign of good luck and smiled before she dozed off.

When Sylvia woke up, she heard a familiar voice. Was it Manola or a dream?

18
FOREIGN LIAISON
By Linda Nash

Jean shut the door behind her and walked briskly down the road, past the terraced houses, some still blacked out, towards the village school. She shivered and pulled her old brown coat more tightly around her, thinking, not for the first time, how wonderful it would be to buy a new one. Alas, this wouldn't be possible, certainly not for the foreseeable future, clothes coupons having to be used for more immediate needs. She strode on pondering her recent promotion to headmistress. She was under no illusions as to it being due to any particular talent on her part, but because the headmaster, who was in his early forties, had been called up to serve in the Army. The promotion was very much a double-edged sword, as she had to continue in her previous job as a school teacher, as well as carrying out the duties of headship, for little extra pay.

She continued down Prospect Road, where the houses were larger and the area more affluent, turned into Kitchener Close, a cul-de-sac, at the end of which was Chiverton Village School. Unlocking the door, she entered quickly, trying not to let the heat escape. The school was heated by a coal-burning stove, which managed to keep the school at a just about bearable temperature. She greeted Mr. Baines, the caretaker, who was opening up the stove prior to filling it with coal.

"Oh it's lovely and warm in here. Thank goodness for the stove."

"Don't know how long for, Miss," said Mr. Baines gloomily. "Soon enough they're bound to start limiting supplies of coal. After all, there are coupons for almost everything, so why not for coal as well?"

Jean smiled.

"Oh, surely not, Mr. Baines. The children have to be kept warm while they are being educated. The Government knows that only too well. Anyway, could we not switch to wood if coal supplies become limited?"

"I suppose we could," he admitted grudgingly. "We're not short of that around here, are we?"

Jean walked down the corridor and opened the door of her classroom. It was painted a bright yellow and the walls were covered with her pupils' work. There were compositions on one wall, pencil drawings on another and brightly coloured paintings on the third. Facing her, there was a large blackboard, taking up almost the entire wall. The shelf below held the chalk and blackboard duster waiting to be used for the next lesson. Jean's desk was in front of the blackboard, facing several rows of the children's wooden two-seater desks.

She shrugged off her coat and hung it on the hook next to the door. She sat at her desk, pulled some exercise books out of her bag, and started looking at the preparations for her first lesson, English. She intended that the children, who varied in ages from 5 to 11, should write a composition on the Nature Study walk they had taken in Chiverton Woods on the previous Tuesday. She wondered whether the enthusiasm they had shown then, was due to the interesting walk, or being out of the classroom for the afternoon.

"Probably a bit of both," she reflected with a wry smile. She was startled by a knocking at her classroom door. She looked at her watch. There was still half an hour before school started.

"Come in and shut the door behind you."

A small fair haired, rather faded looking woman pushed open the door, looking behind her as she closed it, as though she expected someone to be following her. Jean recognised her as the mother of two of her pupils, June and Frank.

"Wondered if I could come and see you, Miss, and ask your advice."

"But, of course, Mrs Smethwick. What can I do to help?"

The woman started off hesitantly, not meeting Jean's eyes, but fixed her gaze on the shelf, below the blackboard.

"Well, it's like this, Miss." she said. "My Frank don't want to come to school no more."

Jean was astonished. "But Frank loves school. He's one of my brightest boys and does well at everything. Added to which, he's popular with the other children."

Mrs Smethwick looked embarrassed, her cheeks turning pink.

"It's not 'is fault," she muttered. "It's all mine," at which she started to cry, silent tears rolling unheeded down her cheeks.

Jean jumped to her feet.

"It can't be as bad as all that," Mrs. Smethwick. "What an earth has happened. Is it to do with your husband? He hasn't been wounded, has he?"

At the mention of her husband, Mrs. Smethwick 's face turned an even deeper shade of pink and the tears became more plentiful.

Suddenly, it came to Jean. She had heard rumours in the village that Mrs. Smethwick had been seen with one of the newly arrived Americans from the local Base. It had to be something to do with that, but she did not want Mrs.

Smethwick to think that she listened to gossip. She placed her hand on the woman's arm.

"As the problem concerns one of my most promising pupils, I need to know exactly what is wrong."

Mrs. Smethwick took a deep breath and looked directly at Jean.

"I've been seeing someone," she admitted. "One of those Yanks from the Air base. I didn't mean to, but I'm so lonely. Our Alf 'as been away now for nearly three years and all I wanted was a bit of grown up company. Elsie Jackson saw me with him. I wasn't doing anything wrong," she added. "But you know what a gossip, she is."

Jean sighed. Although Mrs Smethwick should not have been seeing anyone, she could understand the loneliness. Her boyfriend had also been fighting now for over two years and she missed him dreadfully. Also, Elsie Jackson was just about the biggest and most spiteful gossip in the village. She reflected on Elsie's appearance and the likelihood of anyone being attracted to her. Jealousy probably meant that her gossip was less than truthful. But there was something that she didn't understand.

"I don't quite see how this affects Frank."

Mrs Smethwick started crying again. "Elsie must have told 'er John that I was nothing better than a prostitute and he told the other boys, and they all ganged up on my Frank and said it to him. He came home with his clothes all torn and his face and hands cut and bleeding, where he had fought them, because he thought they were liars."

Jean was alarmed by this last statement. "What do you mean, he thought they were liars? Are you trying to say that," she hesitated, "you have a relationship with this man."

Goodness, she reflected, the Americans have only been here about three weeks.

It was Mrs. Smethwick's turn to look alarmed. "You don't think, oh you mustn't think, no, of course not. We've had a chat a couple of times and he took me to the cafe for a cup of tea. He's lonely too. He's left his wife and little boy behind him in America. It was so nice to talk to someone who understood how I felt."

Suddenly Jean felt very angry. How dare Elsie Jackson. Spreading such spiteful and hurtful rumours. She'd have to nip this in the bud, otherwise goodness knows what it would lead to.

She took hold of Mrs. Smethwick's hands and spoke gently.

"Don't worry. I shall speak to the children, and, if necessary, I will speak to Mrs Jackson," privately hoping that the second course of action would be unnecessary.

"You go on home and try not to worry."

Mrs. Smethwick smiled through her tears.

"Oh, thank you Miss, I can't tell you how relieved I feel."

As she left, Jean glanced at her watch. Only five minutes before school started. The Nature Study composition would have to be postponed. She'd speak to the children during or immediately after Assembly and explain to them how it was possible for men and women from different countries to be friends, and how this friendship could help them to deal with the unhappiness and loneliness caused by being separated from their husbands or wives. It would be naive to think, she reminded herself, that foreign liaisons would always be so innocent, but rumours put about by the likes of Elsie Jackson had to be quashed before any real harm was done.

She sighed as she put on her coat and went out to ring the bell for the children to come in from the playground.

19
A FRIEND FROM THE PAST
By Vesla Small

When Marie drove over the railway bridge, she caught a glimpse of a familiar house. At an age when the past was more real than the future, she wondered about her friend from long-ago who used to live there.

"Parlez-moi d'amour. Redites-moi des choses tendres."

Marie listened to the radio, playing Jean Lenoir's 'Speak to me of love'. She'd often heard Kris sing the song and smiled at the thought of it, reflecting on the good moments they'd spent together.

Kris already had cancer when she first met her. Although heartbroken about the diagnosis, her resolve didn't sway. Witty and smart, Kris was quick with her jokes, turning sadness into gladness. The poems Kris wrote often revealed the solitude she felt after family and friends had turned their backs on her. Kris's stare of loneliness pained Marie, every time she entered her flat in a haze of engrained smoke and the stench of alcohol.

When life became too painful and sad, she resorted to a glass of whisky. "This is to drown my sorrows to forget my tomorrows," she used to say with a hearty chuckle, bringing the glass to her lips.

The illness devoured Kris as a person, and to those who visited her, she was no longer her former self. They had forgotten the Kris they once knew and loved, well hidden inside her sick body. Despite her illness, she saw the funny side of life and often rewarded Marie with a laugh and a good story, based on her own experiences. After a long period of illness, Kris faded away.

Marie continued driving as tears welled up in her eyes.

***

"I'm speaking on behalf of Kris's family, her friends and as her uncle. I knew my niece well. I was present at her birth and watched her grow up. I christened her, married her, christened her children, worked with her and now, I'm here to say farewell to her."

Standing by Kris's coffin, her Uncle dried a tear, looking over the congregation, before he continued.

"Born in 1934 in Bumba on the Congo River, Kris's father was Belgian, a professor in tropical diseases, and her mother was Irish, a licensed midwife.

"I remember Kris as a fresh-faced girl, dimple cheeked and with freckles. Her good sense of humour made it easier when in trouble, and her great strength of character helped her to survive in a brood of five brothers.

"Kris and her brothers learnt the local dialect, Swahili to better bond and understand their native neighbours. The Congolese children joined the siblings during the private tutoring in their home, providing the foundations for mutual respect and friendship. Already at an early age, Kris knew how to share and be supportive of others.

"A lively, astute and passionate person, at eighteen she headed for Louvain in Belgium where she studied to become a nurse. During her studies, she met her future husband, the only child of Belgian parents, also working in the Belgian Congo. After completing their studies, they moved to the northern tip of the Congo River, where they married and had children. They lived and worked there until they left, in the late 1970s, when they realised that their lives were in danger.

"Kris was fearless, hard working, nothing seemed to fluster her. As a mother of three, she sacrificed much of her time in nursing at the Catholic missionary station hospital. Before she started her vocation in life, the poverty and child mortality were high. By the time Kris left the country, she'd been part of the team, making the health service in the Congo the best in the tropical world.

"The values of kindness, involvement and tolerance were essential to Kris. She knew how to take care of the natives, with whom she'd lived ever since her birth. Because there was respect and understanding between them, the Congolese women trusted her and allowed her into their private lives, letting Kris educate them about contraception and hygiene. As a result of Kris's efforts, the child mortality dropped in the region.

"Kris was astute and put up stubborn resistance when someone or something needed her backing. She understood that the only way to change the country for the better was to improve the natives' status. Realising that the inability to read and write was a handicap for the population, Kris helped the Sisters at the station to combat the widespread illiteracy in the area.

"Her resources were limitless, and she worked hard to better people's lives, always with a smile and good humour. Apart from the missionary station's orphanage and hospital, there were no institutions for the widows, the elders and the orphans, so Kris devoted much time to their care.

"Her opinions were insightful and just. Being against segregation of black and white people, Kris mingled with all, and when she and her family left Zaire, heading for Belgium, they arrived with three white and three black children, the latter were children she'd cared for and adopted from the missionary orphan home.

"A happy family with six children started a new life in a Brussels suburb, full of challenges. But, Kris soon realised that in a country where most people have enough to eat and drink, school and healthcare are in hand, peace and stability are reigning, there was no mission waiting for her. Nostalgia caught her, and she often longed for Africa and those she'd cared for.

"Injustice and wrong-doing aroused anger and sadness in Kris. Eventually, she chose two new missions, helping political refugees due to the upheavals in Rwanda and supporting the homeless people in Belgium. Kind, as she was, she dedicated much time to charity work, by raising money to support the weak and destitute, and by being their spokeswoman. Serving other people was the only way Kris could find fulfilment in life.

"Keen to promote the country and its natives, Kris prepared an African museum in the basement of their house, where she exhibited musical instruments, various utensils and pieces of art, originating from the Belgian Congo. Children of all ages visited her museum and learnt from her knowledge of her 'lost' country.

"Many enjoyed the taste of African dishes and drinks she prepared, and several are amongst us today, to pay tribute to Kris.

"Caring for other people gave her life a meaning and a purpose. Kris fought her illness with courage and honour, and she was a model for all. Let peace be with Kris's memory."

Marie smiled to herself, recognising the Uncle that Kris often spoke of. She'd heard many stories about Uncle Vincent as a spiritual leader in the Belgian Congo, where he'd worked a long time. Kris admired and loved him, and judging by the sermon, his feelings and admiration were reciprocal, when sharing Kris's life story with those present.

'That's the Kris I knew and will remember,' thought Marie.

Prayers were said and hymns sung. The priest passed the incense burner over the coffin, sprinkled it with holy water and chanted 'Amen', followed by the sign of the cross.

The organist played Adagio by Albinoni, Kris's much-loved piece of music, filled with emotion, passion and hope, just like the Kris that Marie had known.

Watching the candles around Kris's coffin blow in the draft from the wind coming through the open portal, Marie felt appeased.

Kris had made a lasting impact on Marie, by teaching her the values of friendship and simple things in life, and thereby making her feel rich in heart and mind. Through Kris, Marie gained strength to keep trying and to be hopeful.

She smiled through her tears and thanked her friend.

When Marie turned around, she saw that the congregation livened up. She heard people sniffing and blowing their noses, some nodding and smiling at each other. They'd recognised the caring, and the good humoured personality within the sick body, through Uncle Vincent's sermon. They felt reunited with the Kris they once knew.

20
THE LIFT
By Jake Corey

Belisha Beacon held her Beretta automatic down by her side as she stepped around the side of the kitchen door and into the Karate Kid Sushi Bar. Russ T Bolt, her partner of less than six months, had pleaded with her for him to take the front door. This should have been a walk in the park. The 'terrorist' was a kid of eighteen. He'd found faith and a 'blow you away boom stick' handgun. Why the local cops had called in the FBI was anyone's guess. Babysitting rookies she could handle, but Rusty was past being a rookie. He was an old FBI desk jockey, old enough to be her granddad.

Belisha saw the perp hiding behind the giant fish tank. She felt and smelt his nervousness in the air. Belisha reckoned that if she was lucky, she could ask him to lay down his weapon and come quietly. Then they could get a coffee. She needed it. But that didn't take into account Rusty bursting through the front door, his Smith & Wesson Model 29 hand gun swinging back and forth like an elephant's trunk. He wore his original 1960s suit, which although it may have fitted then, it didn't now. He looked like a sherry trifle squeezed into a hessian bag.

"Come out punk. Come and make friends with 'Dirty Harry'," he roared, imitating a bull elephant with a thorn up its arse.

It would have been laughable if it hadn't been so dangerous.

The perp peaked over the fish tank and made the biggest mistake of his life. He pointed his boom stick at Rusty, who needed no more enticement. Rusty unloaded three rounds through the fish tank and into the kid's chest. The kid wasn't dead, but he would be, soon. His weapon lay, unfired, on the ground near his hand. He lay in the middle of shattered glass and enough flapping fish to keep the sushi bar busy for months.

Rusty kept in character, strolled over to the kid and looked down at him, pointing his S&W at the kid's head. Belisha saw the kid dying for Christ's sake. Sure his hand twitched, but so did the rest of his body.

"Do you feel lucky kid? Well do ya? Go on punk, make my day."

"No, Rusty," Belisha shouted. "The kid's finished."

Blood bubbled from the kid's mouth, amid more twitching. That was enough for Rusty to add another .44 magnum cartridge to the others and end the life of another terrorist.

"He is now. And the free world is safe again," said Rusty, as he holstered his cannon.

***

As they approached the lift in the entrance to FBI headquarters, Belisha saw that as usual, two of the three lifts had signs that read 'Out Of Order'.

Rusty pushed the 'Out Of Order' floor marker out of the way with his foot and tore down the 'Do Not Use!' sign from the wall.

"It's out of order, Rusty," said Belisha.

"Oh yeah. Who says?" said Rusty, with the suave

sophistication of a used-car salesman interviewing for membership of a country club.

Well, thought Belisha, the worst that can happen is the lift gets stuck on the twentieth floor. Following Rusty into the lift, she stood at the back and turned her mind to the story they would have to give their boss, Ewe What. Rusty had been her partner for nearly six months, and she loved him and hated working with him in equal measures. She'd die for him, but she didn't want to die because of him. Belisha had sympathy for Rusty. In a few weeks' time, Rusty could look forward to incontinence and riveting pension conversations with like-minded people, but that was no reason for her to get killed. This should have been Rusty's stroll down memory lane, to a time when bad guys wore black, and the FBI killed them with a smile.

Rusty killed close on a million dollars' worth of fish in the last mission, and the owner of the Karate Kid Sushi Bar threatened to sue. Someone had to explain that to Ewe What. Three more people followed them into the lift, and Rusty pressed the button for the twenty-third floor. One of the other people pressed the button for the twentieth floor, the administration and services floor. From their dress and demeanour, they looked like a janitor and two seasoned secretaries. One wore a face veil, but hey. That's equal rights, right?

Since Rusty had been reassigned to field duties, he eyed everyone with suspicion, and the three fellow travellers were no exception. His eyes narrowed, and his right hand twitched. She hoped that Rusty could control his imagination and avoid killing all of them. They weren't suspicious to her. The three squeezed into the centre of the lift and were intent on not looking at either her or Rusty, although the woman with a face veil may have been Osama Bin Laden for all she knew.

As the lift rose, she heard a banging from beneath the floor, which increased in volume and intensity as the lift passed the third floor. It was metal on metal and increased in intensity as the lift rose. It sounded like someone trapped in the boot of a car just before it went into the car crusher. The three people in the centre looked down and moved around. A secretary tutted as if someone was trying to snatch a peek up her skirt.

Rusty reached behind and under his jacket for his Smith & Wesson. He pulled out the weapon with a speed that would have impressed James Bond, pulled back the hammer and pointed it at the floor, in a two-handed grip.

Belisha wondered what he planned to do with his Dirty Harry cannon in a lift. She wanted to tell him that this was neither the time nor place to practise his quick draw technique. As the face veiled secretary saw the weapon, her eyes bulged, and she screamed, the fabric in front of her mouth bellowing out. The janitor stepped back from Rusty as if he might have Ebola and forced a secretary into a corner behind him.

Whatever possessed Rusty to shoot at the floor, none but the Gods could guess. But discharge two rounds at the metal floor he did. Only a fool would think there was a terrorist under the lift trying to kill them, but Rusty was 'Special'.

Sure enough, as time travelled at a nightmare pace, and events took on a clarity that only an end of life event could evoke, Rusty blasted that lift floor like his life depended on it. Finally, air filled with cordite, Rusty's weapon clicked empty.

In Rusty's defence, the metal against metal hammering stopped, to be replaced by a scream from beneath the floor. There was no mistaking it. It sounded like a repairman, imitating a girl being thrown down a lift shaft.

As Rusty blew smoke from his gun barrel, trained killer style, the floor to the lift dropped away, leaving a shallow lip around the edge, which by good fortune, Belisha and Rusty used to prevent them from disappearing into the shaft.

As the floor clattered down the lift shaft, the janitor

and the face-veiled secretary followed it. The two poor victims dropped with a whoosh, their clothes flapping around them. Belisha concluded that the first victim must have been hit mid repair, while replacing the bolts in the floor. The other two? Well, they were collateral damage.

The repairman's screams ended. Other, equally chilling voices, replaced them. It sounded like a secretary and janitor duet, both sopranos. The lift passed the eight floor as Belisha recognised the thud of the two bodies, impaling themselves on the cables, spikes and machinery at the bottom of the lift shaft.

As she looked up, her eyes met those of the third passenger, the secretary, who with toes barely connecting with the floor edging, slid a hand into her handbag and came out with a small automatic.

Belisha recognised the weapon from FBI basic training as a Soviet made PSS Silent Pistol, a specialist KGB weapon, intended for assassinations and executions. As the weapon appeared, she saw Rusty's eyes register the danger. Belisha knew that if they survived, he'd claim that look was rage, but she knew that it was a combination of fear and the repeating spicy kebab he'd had for lunch.

Who was this assassin's target, Rusty or herself? It was academic she supposed and letting go of the lift railing with one hand, she sliced the woman across the throat with the edge of her hand. The secretary dropped the weapon, which clattered down the shaft.

The secretary gurgled and her hands grasped at her misshapen throat as she regurgitated blood, which hit Rusty in the chest drenching his shirt and jacket. Belisha saw the woman teetering on the edge of the lift toehold, which barely stopped the three of them plunging to their deaths. The secretary assassin teetered on the edge, recognised the danger and grasped at Rusty's tie to save herself, her eyes wide and pleading. As her toes slipped, she took a firm hold on Rusty's tie with both hands and for a second swung in the air, a comic athlete at a circus.

Rusty's face betrayed his fear. Her olfactory evidence supported this conclusion. Belisha imagined both Rusty and the assassin plunging down the lift shaft in a ballet of doom. But Belisha had underestimated Rusty. Reaching down to his ankle, Rusty slid a Fairbairn fighting knife out of its sheath. A knife favoured by the British Army and Royal Marine Commandos, which he'd purchased to support his new field operative status. The thought of saving the injured woman crossed Belisha's mind, but not Rusty's. He sliced through that tie above her hands and the stricken woman fell, the end of the tie grasped firmly in both hands. Unlike the other three doomed victims, this one yodelled with an occasional bang as she connected with the lift shaft wall. The dull thud marked her acquaintance with the other martyrs.

The lift continued to the twenty-third floor and as the doors opened, Rusty fell back landing on his right shoulder, rolled onto his back and lay still. Half in and half out of the lift, his right arm crossed over his body, his jacket sleeve soaking up the secretary's blood, Rusty looked every bit the wounded secret agent in a Bond film. As Belisha crept around the edge of the lift, she faced three FBI agents pointing snub-nosed .38 revolvers at her.

Belisha gasped, "Special Agents Russ T Bolt and Belisha Beacon. The assassin is below," she said, pointing down the lift shaft.

As the paramedics strapped Rusty to the stretcher, the three agents holstered their weapons and cuffed Belisha, to be on the safe side.

***

Belisha sat in her glass office booth typing the final edit to the report on how they'd terminated an innocent repairman under the lift, a secretary and a janitor. She looked up, over her glasses and grimaced as her colleagues cheered outside. Rusty strolled along the corridor, his arm in a sling as he sucked up the applause and slaps on the back.

She saw him wag his finger at someone and tell them to watch his injured arm, laugh, then pretend to shoot the guy with two fingers.

"Hey Rusty, get in here and bring your sidekick Belisha Beacon with you," shouted What.

Belisha slipped her glasses off, dropped them on the desk and grabbed a folder and pen. They'd both be fired. She'd even cleared her desk drawers and eaten the last of the chocolate digestives she'd found from two years back.

"Let me do the talking right?" she said to Rusty, who had an ear-to-ear grin on his face.

"No problem, baby. It's horses for courses," said Rusty.

"What? What are you talking about, you moron?" said Belisha, confused.

He spread his arm wide and grinned at her, "Hey baby, I do the killin' and you do the typin' and talkin'. Natural selection, sweetheart."

"But...but," she spluttered. "Never mind. Get in there and keep quiet," she said as she pushed Rusty in the back and through the door to Ewe What's office.

"Sit," said What.

That was a bad sign. Everyone knew that you only got to 'sit' if the boss wanted to fire you, gently.

What sat forward in his seat, his hands clasped in front of him, a huge grin on his face. "Coffee?" he asked.

"No thanks. I'm good," said Belisha.

"Yes please, make mine a flat white and plenty of sugar and maybe a biscuit or two, will ya boss?"

"Sure Rusty," said What.

He pressed a button on the intercom and bawled the order, then turned back to the pair. Ewe What was tense, under pressure.

"You sure made a scene yesterday," the words hissed through clenched teeth.

"Ewe, I can explain," Belisha started.

A stubby finger jabbed in her direction. "No explanation, Belisha. I don't want to hear it from you."

He turned his gaze on Rusty, and his expression softened. "Rusty, outstanding, awesome. How did you know that the woman coming up in the lift was a terrorist and the most-wanted female assassin on the FBI's Wanted List?"

Belisha stared at her partner like a zombie had sucked her brain out.

"Gee Boss, intuition I guess. After decades of studying terrorists, I have a natural instinct. What I can't figure is, why she was coming to this floor."

Rusty rubbed his chin in confusion as if he'd been up all night trying to crack the case.

"Intel informs me she was on her way to kill yours truly."

"What?" asked Belisha, coughing and finally finding her voice. "What?"

"That's right, Belisha. What, that's me. Ewe What. She'd walk right in here, kill me with her silent pistol and walk straight out. As casual as you please."

"But...Ewe," Belisha was speechless, again.

"Belisha, look, stop that spluttering thing. It makes you sound stupid."

He turned back to Rusty as the coffee arrived. "Here's the coffee, and it's well deserved. Sorry about the injury, Rusty. You'll get compensation of course. I've recommended you for a commendation for bravery. Not you, Belisha. If it hadn't been for Rusty, you'd both be dead and me too. I'm recommending that Rusty continue in the service, and that he retrain you."

"What happened to the other victims, Ewe? The other dead guys?" asked Rusty.

"Trust you to think of other people Rusty. Compassion as well." What shook his head in admiration. "In wartime combat casualties are acceptable. Belisha, you should learn a lesson here. Keep your eyes open and try to spot the tell-tale signs. Got it?"

Belisha nodded open mouthed.

"God, I love this job, Ewe. It's what I've been training for all my life," said Rusty.

Ewe What stood and pressed both fists on his desk and looked at Belisha. "Hear that Belisha? He loves his job. Now go do the typing or something. I need to go over the fine details with Rusty and how he spotted this terrorist. Leave us to do the man talk. You are dismissed."

Belisha left the room, her head bowed, her hands hanging limp, a scolded child. She'd missed something but for the life of her, she couldn't see what.

21
THE ADVENTURER
By Vesla Small

'Here comes my sunshine,' she thought, as her grandson ran towards her.

First they kissed and then holding hands, the two set off for a day of adventures. Her grandson carried his rucksack on his back and looked to the world like a little adventurer.

'How he's grown,' she thought, remembering holding him soon after his birth and feeling a powerful connection. He was her first grandchild, so special.

"Got tickets, Kemor?" asked her grandson.

She nodded and smiled.

He toddled along, looking up at her with beaming eyes. They were about to travel by train to Brussels-Midi railway station, and he was filled with excitement for the trip ahead, with his Bestemor.

"Kemor, hurry, we miss train!" he seemed eager, almost impatient.

She smiled when he said, "Kemor," the best he could manage for Bestemor, Norwegian for grandmother. 'He'll get there in time,' she smiled to herself.

Two strong arms lifted him up the high steps into the

train. The cheerful bearded ticket collector ruffled his soft hair and wished him a pleasant trip. She followed the two, with a firm grip on her handbag.

After they'd settled down on a bench by the window, he eagerly opened his rucksack and pulled out two biscuits, one for Bestemor and one for him. Whilst they drank water and munched biscuits, they watched the world fly by.

"Kemor, we're on a train, like Thomas!" His eyes gleamed with delight.

Her grandson loved the stories she read to him about Thomas the Tank Engine and his Friends.

"Thomas goes slowly and Diesel goes very fast. Is this one fast, Kemor?" there was an inkling of nervousness in his voice.

She fell into step with her grandson and lost herself in his four-year old world. The rhythmic sound from the train seemed soothing. Some passengers, walking by, stopped for a moment and smiled at the couple.

"Kemor, look, a long train!" he sounded impressed.

"That's Eurostar, a very fast train," she told him.

As he looked out of the window, he asked in anticipation, "Are we there yet?"

His innocent smile warmed her heart, and she put her arm around him, "Soon, quite soon."

She'd always loved trains, the sound and the feeling of them, and the ever changing view through the train windows. Now, she had someone to share her passion with. 'It must be in the genes,' she thought, her lips curled into a smile.

They arrived, and the same ticket collector lifted the young passenger from the train and down on the platform. "Enjoy your day trip. Look after your grandma, little man. Mind your handbag, Madam. This is a busy railway station."

"Hold on to my hand, all the time. Don't let go of it," she said, as they found their way between busy travellers.

"Yes, Kemor," he answered.

Her grandson seemed overwhelmed by the sounds, the smells and the chaotic atmosphere that surrounded them.

"Look! There's the escalator. Do you want to walk down the stairs or take the escalator?" she asked.

"Escalator, please, Kemor," he gave her a shy smile, and pulled her toward the escalator.

She'd told him about the many escalators and lifts on the railway station, and he was convinced that escalators were magic.

Her thoughts went back to when she and her brother visited the biggest store in Oslo and travelled up and down the escalators in Steen & Strøm. It was probably the only escalator in the country, and it was the first time they'd been on one. They'd been up and down several times, when their mother heard the announcement over the loudspeakers, "Will the parents of the two children running on the escalators, kindly look after them."

Those were fond memories, and she smiled, as she gazed at her grandson who, for the first time, experienced the real world of trains and crowds of people.

"Be careful. Hold my hand while we step on the moving stairs," she looked him in the eyes, demanding his full attention. To take a young child to a busy, cosmopolitan railway station could be risky, but the same went for the escalators, and she had no desire to get into difficulty.

He nodded and pulled her hand to make her walk faster. She helped him on to the moving stairs, and his first trip down an escalator began. Whilst he looked down the moving stairs, his handgrip tightened. Once they'd stepped off the escalator, his little face broke into a smile. Was it relief or victory?

"Did you like that?"

"Yes," he nodded and pulled her arm, as he pointed in the opposite direction. "Go other way now... Please?"

"Yes, dear, but first let's have something to eat and

drink at Sam's Café."

He loved going to a café with his Bestemor and followed her. As they strolled along, he was over the moon watching the escalators. There were so many of them, more than he could count.

As they waited in the queue, he stared at the lady behind the counter with scribbles over her arms and rings in her lip, until he heard his Bestemor saying, "Pain au chocolat, croissant, coffee and water."

Beaming, he asked for 'pain au chocolat', his favourite.

"Where do you want to sit?" she asked, as she balanced the tray, keeping an eye on her grandson.

"There, near zebra," her grandson responded, and walked faster.

The two settled at the table next to the giant zebra in wax. While she took a photo of her grandson with the zebra in the background, a tramp came to their table.

"A coin to spare, please?" he asked, and stretched out the rough palm of his hand.

She watched her grandson's reaction.

"Kemor, man forgot money at home?" his voice sounded innocent.

She smiled, put a coin in his hand, and asked him to give it to the man. The stranger thanked them and continued to stagger along the vast passage.

"Before we try the escalators again, we need to visit the toilet," she said, and packed up their belongings.

Holding her grandson's hand, they walked leisurely along the hall. When they reached the facilities, and she wanted to pay the attendant, she realised that her handbag was gone. She panicked, but remembered that she'd put her personal papers in the inside pocket of her coat, together with a ten euro note.

Once they'd done their errand, they walked back to Sam's Café, where they saw the same old man sitting at the table they'd left.

As he saw them, he called, "You left your handbag on

this chair, Madam. Nothing has been taken."

"I walk up and down this hall most of the day to keep myself warm. I'm more fragile than I used to be. If I'm lucky, I may get money off strangers, but rarely," he mumbled, and handed her the handbag, giving her a gap-toothed grin.

She smiled back. "How silly of me. It must be age, too many things to think of. Thank you," she said and sat at his table, with her grandson on her lap.

He looked at them, saying, "I also have a grandson, somewhere in Belgium. I haven't seen him since his birth. His name's Lucas, a lovely baby."

A tear ran down his wrinkled face, she felt sorry for him, and thought. 'God acts in ways we don't understand.'

"If you don't mind, I'd like to buy something for you to eat," she offered.

"No, thank you," he replied. "I receive food from the municipal soup kitchen. I've been going there for years. It fills a hole... I wouldn't mind a beer though."

She brought him a glass of beer and pressed money into his hand. "Thank you, again. I hope you'll meet your grandson. Grandchildren are wonderful. They fill our hearts and make us whole," she smiled, and left him to his own devices.

"A good man, Kemor?" the little one asked, as they waved to him, on their way to platform eighteen.

As she walked, she felt her grandson pull her hand more than needed.

"Faster, Kemor, faster!" he said, and giggled.

His laughter was contagious and again, she lost herself in her grandson's four-year old world.

They'd spent a little time on the escalators when she realised that the station clock showed three. It was time to go home.

"One more time on the 'magic carpet' to the Eurostar platform," she proposed.

When they reached the platform, they watched people

entering the high-speed train.

"Not going on fast train, are we, Kemor?"

Once more, she sensed a slight nervousness in his voice. She realised that despite travelling up and down the escalators and seeing the trains coming and going, he wasn't quite into speed, yet.

"No, dear, we'll go on the slow train back home," she said, and put her arms around him.

Relieved, he cuddled up to her.

"Before we take the train, let's buy a present for mummy," she suggested.

Once more they strolled along the station's huge hall, once more they went to the toilets, and once more they met the tramp, before they went on the train.

There was a big smile on his little face when he spotted the same cheerful, beard-faced ticket collector. He proudly showed him the red rose, "Present for my mummy."

When they reached their destination, her daughter was waiting for them. And as her grandson ran into his mother's arms, she smiled, 'There goes my sunshine.'

22
THE TRAMP
By Linda Nash

The tramp leaned on his shopping trolley, peering intently through the window of the furniture shop. Pulling up the collar of his shabby tweed coat, he wrapped his woolly scarf more tightly around his neck and tried to pull his battered trilby hat further over his ears. Hunching into his coat, trying to protect himself from the biting February wind, he looked longingly at the beautiful furniture, suddenly catching sight of a gilt pendulum clock, with an intricately decorated face. The tramp started, realising that the clock was almost the same as the one before ... The tramp stopped his thoughts immediately. 'There's no point even going there,' he told himself.

Reluctantly, he moved away from the window, wearily making his way towards a hostel, which was about half a mile away, down the Clerkenwell Road in the City. With luck he could probably get a bed there for the night, and if not, well he would have to make do with a park bench or a doorway. He didn't relish the thought of a night out in the February cold, although he had covers enough in his trolley.

This time he was in luck, managing to acquire one of

the last free beds in the hostel, and to his relief was able to have a shower and a shave. He kept himself to himself, no point allowing yourself to be drawn into a conversation. People always asked you questions, and answering them was for him anyway, too revealing and too painful. 'The past is the past,' he told himself, 'and as far as I'm concerned, that's where it will stay.'

Nevertheless, his thoughts kept returning to the clock he had seen in the furniture shop. John tried his utmost to push away the painful memories that returned with the image. Eventually, exhaustion took over and he fell asleep, and then in no time at all he was jerked awake by the noise of the hostel. He ate some cereal and a slice of bread and before 9 o'clock, he was pushing his trolley along the Clerkenwell Road towards St Pancras Station. There he could get away from the cold and hopefully passersby would take pity on him and give him a few coins. Near the taxi rank was a good spot, as foreign tourists on their way home nearly always had English cash they wanted to get rid of. John walked quite briskly, but then he was only in his early forties and on closer inspection, it could be seen that he was a good looking man, with piercing blue eyes and a thick crop of dark hair, liberally sprinkled with white.

Somehow, he was drawn again to that same furniture shop window. He leaned on his trolley, promising himself that it would only be for a minute, and again he looked intently into the shop, his eyes immediately homing in on the wall clock. As he did so he became aware that someone inside the shop was staring out at him. Instinctively, he looked down and started to walk away, before he could be moved on. As he reluctantly pushed his trolley away from the shop, he heard a voice behind him addressing him.

"It's John Curtis, isn't it? No don't go, I'm sure it's you. We've all been trying to find you for ages."

The tramp turned around and looked at the man, who too was in his early forties. He was also good looking, but the difference was in his dress. The man was wearing a smart, well cut, navy blue suit with a bright pink shirt and a matching pink and grey striped tie, not a regimental one, John was pleased to note. The man was also smiling at him, something that didn't happen too often. It was then that he recognised him. It was Toby Marshall. What was he doing here? Of course, Toby's father had a whole string of furniture shops. Toby had always sworn that he would never work for his father, "but there you go, never is a long time." Still, Toby was a good man, "the bravest of the brave," and had always looked out for him.

"Yes, you're right," he said reluctantly. "It's me, John Curtis." Saying his name felt strange. Since becoming a tramp, he had used John Brown, as this, he felt, made it much less likely that he would be recognised or found. He turned away instinctively, Toby Marshall was part of his past and that was all behind him now and he wasn't ready or willing to face it. But Toby had anticipated that and was now facing him and had put a restraining hand on his arm.

"Don't go, John. Don't run away again. All your friends, me included, have been trying to find you, ever since we heard about Jane and Emily, but all our letters were returned and our telephone calls went unanswered. Please come inside and at least have a cup of tea or coffee and listen to what I have to say."

John looked up at Toby. He saw the concern and kindness in his friend's face. After all, what harm could a cup of something warm do, it would allow him to sit down and kill a little time, if nothing else. Time was what you had too much of when you were a tramp. John followed Toby into the shop, feeling the curious eyes of the assistants on him.

They went into the office and Toby pushed forward an armchair, probably intended for clients or prospective clients. John sank into it, appreciating the softness of the material and the way it fitted his body. It seemed like an eternity since he had enjoyed such luxury. He felt himself, albeit unwillingly, relaxing. Toby was speaking.

"How about a cup of tea, or would you prefer coffee?"

"Coffee," he replied, without thinking. "A black coffee would be wonderful." How long had it been since he had indulged in the luxury of a real cup of coffee, not that awful instant stuff that the 'do gooders' thought was good enough for the likes of tramps and down and outs.

Toby called in one of his assistants, a tall, pretty girl with long black curly hair.

"Jane, could you get us both a black coffee and perhaps a couple of cakes or pastries to go with them?"

As Jane walked out of the office, Toby turned to John, who had gone pale and was trembling.

"What is it, old chap? Are you ill?" Then he realised. "It's because her name's Jane, isn't it?

John nodded, not daring to speak. Tears were running down his face. Crying was something he had had also firmly relegated to the past, shortly after Jane, his beloved Jane, had been taken away from him.

Toby handed him a handkerchief and he gratefully wiped his eyes.

Toby spoke to him gently. "You have to stop running away, John. You've got to face your demons and get on with your life. You've been a tramp for," he paused, as he calculated, "must be about two years?"

John nodded. He was frightened that if he spoke, he would break down again.

Toby looked up as Jane brought in the coffee and cakes and put them on the desk.

"Thanks so much, Jane." She and Toby smiled at each other and John sensed that there was something more between them than a friendly employer, employee relationship.

Toby handed him his cup of coffee and offered him a cake, which John accepted. You didn't refuse food, as you never knew when you would eat again.

They drank and ate in silence, and then Toby spoke

again. "Philip Willoughby, James Chalmers, Derek Smithers and I, want to help you. No, just hear me out," he said, as John opened his mouth to protest.

"Look at yourself, John, you're a clever man. You entered the Army full of talent and promise. For several years that talent was put to good use and you were quickly promoted. Then came the horrors of Iraq, followed by those of Afghanistan. As if that wasn't enough for you to bear, seeing your friends and colleagues killed and maimed, when you left the Army and returned home to lick your wounds, your wife and young daughter were killed in a car accident. You need proper help, and by that I mean some sort of psychiatric or psychological treatment in agreeable and supportive surroundings. We've found somewhere for you to stay, which helps veterans from Iraq and Afghanistan to face their traumas and get back on their feet. It's in Hampshire, not far from where James Chalmers lives. It will take you at least six months and maybe even longer to recover, but you owe it to both Jane and Emily to do so, not mentioning your friends, of course," he added, with a smile. "The Army will fund your treatment. What do you say?"

John sat there in silence, his mind churning. He felt weariness overtake him, and he could barely keep his eyes open. All this running away had sapped his energy. All he wanted to do was lie down and go to sleep. It was even an effort to speak.

"I'd like to think about it," he said finally. "Suddenly I feel exhausted."

Toby was concerned. "Of course. Meeting me again, must have been a shock for you. I'll run you over to my flat. I live on my own, so you'll have all the peace and quiet you need. I'll be back at lunch time to get us something to eat. I'll just go and tell the staff I have to leave for an hour or so."

John waited for Toby to return, trying to fight the rising feeling of panic at the thought of what lay before him, if he fell in with his friend's plan. Did he really want to go down that road? It would mean having to face all that horror and grief again. He started to get up, but then sank back into the chair. How much longer could he continue as he was, aimlessly drifting and relying on charity? Toby was right. He owed it to Jane and Emily to get back on his feet.

John looked up to see Toby in the doorway, smiling at him. Suddenly, he felt the return of his old resolve. He got to his feet.

"Lead on Macduff," he said. Then, straightening his shoulders he walked determinedly through the back of the shop, across the car park, and climbed into Toby's car.

23
THE PRISONER
By Jake Corey

"Come on, the Governor wants to see you today, you lazy individual," shouted Mr Lockart, the Chief Warder, turning puce.

Regardless of Lockart's attempt at coercion, Bradley Maudlin was in no hurry. He shuffled along the corridor, a dirty gloss painted wall on one side that may once have been white, but was now various shades of filth and cigarette smoke, and a guardrail on the other, intended to stop the likes of him from throwing themselves to the ground, thirty metres below. Maudlin wondered whether Lockart might try to stop him. He thought not, he might even hold his jacket.

At the sound of Lockart's voice, two inmates looked up. Maudlin tried not to pay attention, but knew that it was Josey's pool playing time. Maudlin stopped and looked down at the two men. Lockart prodded him with his pace stick. The story was that Mr Lockart had been an RSM in the Military Detention Centre. His nickname was either Lockjaw or Lockart the Tart depending on which gave the inmates the most amusement.

Maudlin ignored the prod and stood, thinking. If he

was going to do it, it had to be now. No hesitation. Right now. Left foot onto the lower rail, right foot on the top and over he'd go. He looked down at the two men, their upturned faces contorted like two twisted blackthorn branches, dark, dangerous, and painful if spiked.

"Did you enjoy last night in the shower, old son?" shouted Josey.

Urged on by his boss's excited squeal, Runner slid the pool cue between his legs and made an obscene gesture.

"See you in the exercise yard, Bradley. We can make beautiful music, baby," he imitated Maudlin's clipped and prissy tone.

Runner gyrated his hips, using the pool cue so that he resembled a grotesque pole dancer. Josey and Runner broke into fits of laughter. A few seconds later, Josey thumped Runner playfully and motioned for him to take his shot at the pool table. Maudlin was a source of amusement but a disposable memory until tonight, when he'd be a source of release from their hormonal tension.

Maudlin imagined himself falling the thirty metres to the ground, spread-eagled, like Batman descending onto an unsuspecting rogue. If he was lucky, he'd land on both, ending their meaningless lives. If he didn't hit them, at least he'd land on the pool table and upset their game. But if they survived, they'd enjoy hours of fun in the retelling and it would legitimise their game. In the countless telling, they'd exaggerate and embellish the story. It would be like a burlesque theatre production. He looked at his hands on the rail, his knuckles were white, bloodless, shaking. Lockart shouted something but he may well have been reciting Shakespeare for all Maudlin cared. He leaned further out over the rail, almost doubled over, a shock of black hair falling over his face. He was above the two men. Maudlin focused on Runner's bald patch he'd attempted to comb over. Josey who was about to take a shot reminded him of a squeezed doughnut. If he waited until Josey had taken his shot, he might land on both. The pool cue came back then smacked the white ball with a crack, ricocheting around the prison like a gunshot, which spurred Maudlin into action. Left foot on the bottom rail and a firm grip on the top rail. The two men below exchanged a few words, their heads only a few inches apart. This was it, the end. He was calm, serene. He put his weight on the rail and was about to shove off when he felt the handcuff slide around his wrist and rattle on the top rail. Looking at his hands still grasping the rail, he realised that Lockart must have guessed his plan and handcuffed him to the rail. The last thing he wanted was to be left hanging by one wrist, only to provide yet more hours of entertainment for the inmates.

The moment, the opportunity to free himself from his decomposing life and to end those of his tormenters, passed. It was a winning lottery ticket except that the 'valid until' date had passed. He couldn't even top himself.

"Not on my watch, sonny. My pension's due soon."

He forced himself to let go of the railing but now handcuffed to the Chief Warder, he shuffled along the corridor to the Governor's office, Lockart's steel tipped boots making tiny tip taps on the concrete floor. As they stood outside the office, Lockart looked Maudlin up and down as if inspecting a soldier to meet the Queen. He 'humphed' his dissatisfaction.

"That is too easy. I'm here to make sure society gets payback. You ... you ... girl," he spat out the last word as if there was no greater insult and Maudlin supposed that for a man of his limited ability and bigoted disposition it was.

Lockart unlocked the handcuffs and Maudlin wiped his hand across his hair. He felt like a small boy waiting to see the headmaster. Lockart rapped once on the solid wooden door.

"Come," echoed from inside the room.

Lockart pushed the door open, giving Maudlin a push in the back.

"510670 Maudlin Bradley, Governor, sir," said Lockart standing to one side, his final mission accomplished, he'd saved the world, his chest the size of a buffalo.

"Thank you, Mr Lockart. You may leave us," said the Governor dismissively.

After a pause the door closed and Maudlin imagined Lockart's vexation. He kept his eyes downcast until he realised that there were two voices behind the desk, unless the Governor had taken up ventriloquism. Maudlin had never seen the Governor before but guessed that he was the smiley looking man with the Oxfam suit. The man sitting next to him tapped his pen on the folder in front of him, his eyes darted to Maudlin and back to the Governor. Maybe visiting a prison unnerved him. Perhaps he thought that associating with criminals might make him one too.

"Maudlin, please sit. I've sent for you because we have news I must break to you."

Maudlin considered this statement. 'news I must break to you'. That implied bad news. He wondered what could be bad news in his present circumstance. A transfer to another prison maybe? Even the Governor couldn't be oblivious to Maudlin's torment, surely? Solitary confinement? But what was this other, nervous little chap doing here? Perhaps someone had planted drugs in his cell and this character was a policeman. He didn't have the build for one. If he was, he'd be less unctuous and subservient to the Governor. Maudlin shook from the episode in the corridor and didn't concentrate on the words flowing across the desk.

"...yesterday, I'm afraid. Mr Upwhistle is your father's solicitor. He's here to give you the details. I thought it best to do everything at once, get it over with."

"What?" said Maudlin, looking at the two men as if they'd spontaneously appeared from another planet.

"Mr Upwhistle, please be so kind."

"Mr Maudlin, Mr Templeton Maudlin your father that is, died in his sleep last night. The cause of death is unclear. However, he may have had a heart attack. I've been his solicitor for a few years and I will administer and execute his will. We are sorry for your loss and please accept my condolences."

"And mine, of course," added the Governor, too quickly.

They looked across at Maudlin for his reaction. He leaned forward in his straight-backed chair until his chin touched his knees and his hair flopped down covering his face. His shoulders trembled and he let out a soft mewing sound. His father was dead, the old man dead. He'd come to think of his father as eternal, always there to persecute him. There'd be no more of his incessant talk of the honourable profession of Funeral Directors, burials and embalming. No more entombing magazines to be pawed over and litter the house, no more father figure to look up to and despise. His ghost would be laid to rest. He was finally free to sell up and blow the lot. His mind leapt, a butterfly dancing on buttercups. All thoughts of the evening's planned abasement at the hands of Josey and his friends disappeared. Even the past pain was a distant memory. He'd bide his time, smile as they accosted him. The feeble-minded scumbags could enjoy and crush his body. Given time that might heal, but once out of prison he'd be a man of means. And if Templeton Maudlin could see him, he'd know the meaning of squander. A lesson in having a good time. For his local would be The Ritz. The waiter, expecting him, would prepare Dom Pérignon on ice for him to brisk like water.

He was brought back to reality, by a nudge at his shoulder. Maudlin saw the glass of water offered by the Governor. As Maudlin looked up, the Governor's expression changed faster than a kangaroo sitting on a cattle prod. One second he was a kindly pen pusher offering sympathy and water. The next, seeing Maudlin's manic grin, he seemed to be on the verge of a stroke.

Maudlin was cackling, he looked at Upwhistle, "Go on,

how much is the place worth? Don't say he left it all to charity." Maudlin wiped tears of joy from his eyes with a blue serge sleeve.

"Your father indicated that he had every intention of changing his will and leaving the majority of his considerable wealth to charity. Nevertheless, his passing away preceded the realisation of the actuality."

"So, it's mine yeah?"

"In a manner of speaking. There is a codicil to the will. A condition, most specific."

"Do go on, Upwhistle. Can't wait."

Upwhistle looked over his glasses at Maudlin, looking concerned in a manner only elderly solicitors can master. He cleared his throat. "Do you wish me to read it out or give you the gist of it, Mr Maudlin?"

"Just tell me."

"The whole of the assets and interests are invested in the funeral business and are bequeathed to you, Mr Maudlin. On condition you carry on the said business and take up the profession of Funeral Director after a suitable course of training to be determined by White and Wetlock, in spirit and actuality, and thereby follow in your father's footsteps."

Maudlin's face dropped. He slumped. He knew his father. The clause had to be watertight. That was the nature of the old bastard.

"Yeah, but there's a get out of jail free card, right?"

Upwhistle shook his head, causing his jowls to wobble with enough vigour to shake the desk upon which he placed his elbows.

"If you mean is there a way of circumventing that clause, certainly not, I'm pleased to say. You see, Mr Maudlin, I drafted the will. If you fail to complete the training or carry on your father's business as its head and in accordance with his intention, all funds and assets will go to the state."

"Bloody hell. Who's this 'White and Wetlock'? Can't

we do a deal?"

"Mr Maudlin, I am the senior partner in White and Wetlock and we certainly can't 'do a deal'."

Upwhistle spat out the last few words as if a stubborn apple pip was stuck in his false teeth.

"How long?"

"If you mean how long must you run the business before you are relieved, the law might interpret that as from the time you are discharged from this establishment to when you are either mentally or physically incapable. Of course, that determination is at my, or my successor's, adjudication. Are there any questions? I can provide the full transcript for your perusal."

Maudlin was speechless. No fortune, no good time, simply a lifetime of misery and dealing with the dead. He thought back to his fleeting plan to end his life prematurely and regretted his hesitation.

24
THE VISIT
By Linda Nash

The young boy stood on the steps, shoulders bent, hugging his bag to his chest, while the rain ran down his face, dripping off his dark hair onto his pullover, making it cling to his slender body. He wore shabby jogging pants and on his feet worn out trainers. His rather unkempt appearance suggested an orphan, or at the very least, a child whose mother showed little interest in his appearance. The door behind him opened and John, the social worker in charge of his group, looked out.

"Come back in Joe. Your Granny will be here soon and she knows where to find you, doesn't she?"

The boy turned round, his eyes deep brown pools of anxiety. Surely Granny wouldn't let him down, would she? The only time she hadn't come was when she was ill and then she'd telephoned to let him know. He'd cried because he was disappointed, not because she had let him down, but because he would have to wait longer to see her. But with grownups you never could be sure, could you? Reluctantly, he walked up the steps into the hall, where he stood, unsure as to what he should be doing. John handed him a towel to dry himself as best he could. As he handed

John the towel, he heard the office phone ringing. Perhaps that was Granny saying she couldn't come. He felt the familiar churning in his stomach and blinked hard to stop any stray tears trying to escape. He didn't want the others calling him a sissy.

John had gone into the office to answer the phone. He was smiling so it couldn't be bad news, could it? He put the phone down, locked the office door and came over to Joe, putting his arm round the boy's shoulders.

"That was Granny," he said. "She had a problem with her car, so she is coming to fetch you in Grandad's. She should be here in about ten minutes."

Joe felt a warm feeling of relief gradually replacing the churning in his stomach. He beamed at John, who hugged him, knowing from experience how it had been for the boy. Sadly, Joe was not alone in this. The majority of his charges were prey to unreliable parents, making careless promises they rarely kept. These young people had no choice but to live in an institution, split into several groups of about twenty boys, each separated by age. These groups were called, in his opinion, rather euphemistically, 'family groups.' Sometimes the boys were there because of a severe handicap, but more often than not, it was inadequate parenting. In Joe's case it was a feckless mother, who had loved him as a baby, but was unable to cope with him growing up. She had seen various doctors and psychiatrists, saying that he was out of control and should be prescribed pills to calm him down. Joe had been taking pills from the age of five and was placed in a boarding school at age seven. Apparently, his visits home during this part of his life had been, to say the least, spasmodic. His mother pleaded illness on many occasions and let him down constantly. She had withdrawn him from boarding school, seemingly on a whim, and he had gone to live at home with her and her current boyfriend. This had resulted in poor attendance at school, a lack of parental guidance and finally in him being taken into care. Through all this at least, his grandmother had remained a constant in his turbulent young life.

The sound of a car driving into the grounds interrupted John's thoughts. Joe grabbed his bag, pushed open the door and ran to the car. He rushed to hug his grandmother as she stepped out.

"Granny, I was worried you weren't coming," he said his voice quavering.

His Granny looked at him in surprise. "But Joe I'd have let you know if I couldn't come." She smiled at him, knowing only too well the reason for his anxiety. "Get in and I'll go and say hello to John before we leave."

Having confirmed with John that she would return Joe at seven, she hurried back to the car, where he was sitting in the front, already buckled up awaiting her. Smiling at him, she apologised again for being late.

"Don't worry, Granny, you were a bit late but it doesn't matter," he said, wanting to reassure her. She knew it did, but didn't press the point.

They had been driving for a few minutes, when he said, as he always did, "What are we having for lunch?"

She described the shepherd's pie she had made, knowing it was one of his favourites, and told him that Granddad was probably, at that moment, preparing carrots, which were about the only vegetable Joe would eat. Dessert was rice pudding, also a favourite of his.

"Which way would you like to drive home?" she asked, as they approached the crossroads.

"Along by the canal, Granny. We might be lucky enough to see a barge."

As they approached the canal, Joe craned his neck and to his obvious delight spotted a barge making its ponderous way up the canal towards the lock.

"Would you like me to stop?" said his Granny.

"Oh would you?" asked Joe eagerly.

He had once confided in her that he'd like to work on a barge when he grew up. In Joe's life dreams and hope for the future were essential. She had seized this opportunity to encourage him to work hard at school, in order that he could make his dreams come true.

She stopped the car and they went to stand at the guardrail, bordering the canal. They watched as the barge slowly made its way past them. They could see a man in the cockpit, driving, and a lady cleaning on the outside deck. They waved to her, and she stopped working for a moment and waved back. There was a car at the back of the barge and Joe wondered how they managed to get it onto dry land. His Granny pointed to a hoist at the rear of the barge and explained that this would be attached to the car, which would then be swung onto the side of the canal. They continued watching until the barge was almost out of sight. Granny looked at her watch and gasped.

"Goodness me, Joe, if we don't want burnt shepherd's pie and soggy carrots, without mentioning a cross Granddad, I think we'd better get a move on, don't you?"

Joe laughed. He loved his Granny's jokes and the way her face lit up when she looked at him.

She waited for him to say what he always said as they approached home. "Poppy will be pleased to see me, won't she?"

"Of course, she looks forward to your visits."

This too, was another constant in his life, another security blanket, a loving dog, always waiting to greet him. She thought sadly how little it took to make him happy and how fragile was his happiness.

"We're almost there," he shouted as they turned the corner into the road where his grandparents lived.

As soon as the car stopped, Joe jumped out, running down the path towards the dog bounding towards him.

"Poppy, Poppy," he shouted, as the dog jumped up, licking his face. "Have you missed me?"

Patiently his Granny gave her usual reply.

"Of course, look how she greets you. She doesn't do that to everybody, you know."

Joe sat down beside Poppy, stroking her and sucking his thumb, so she went into the kitchen, where her husband was finishing the preparations for lunch.

"Sorry we're a bit late," she said, "but we were barge watching."

"How is he?" asked Joe's Granddad.

"Pretty well the same as usual," she replied. "Except that when I arrived, his anxiety was almost palpable. I felt badly about being late."

"Don't go there," he said. "You've never knowingly let him down."

She sighed. "I know, but it's so awful seeing him that way."

Just then Joe came into the kitchen, asking if there was anything he could do. He was given the table to set. When he called his grandmother to check, she noticed that once again he had laid the knives and forks back to front. When he asked her if they were the right way round, she shook her head and he changed them, adding ruefully that he never managed to get it right.

She reassured him that it wasn't important, it was probably because his Mummy was left handed. She had to tell Joe to wait for everybody to be served before he started his meal. His table manners were almost non-existent, but as he was only there for the day and not wanting to make mealtimes into a battleground, they had chosen to concentrate on their own plates. He shovelled the food into his mouth, spilling equal quantities on himself and on the table, but they said nothing as they felt that his visits should be as free from conflict as possible. Joe was over eager to please, apologising profusely for the slightest mistake, as though he feared not being able to come again.

The meal over, Joe wanted to know what was planned for the afternoon. As the weather was sunny and dry, he was asked whether he would like to go for a walk in the woods with Poppy. His beaming face confirmed his approval. He wanted to leave immediately, but was persuaded that his grandparents first needed a cup of tea and ten minutes rest. While waiting, he went into the sitting room and switched on the television.

They raised their eyebrows, but at ten Joe had not yet learned to read and write. A cocktail of poor attendance at school, pills and constant anxiety where his mother was concerned, had meant that his concentration was poor. His teacher at the Home had confided in his grandmother that the schooling Joe received was only a few hours a day and often Joe did not apply himself. He preferred to play around and distract the others, unless it was something that caught his imagination, and then he would work hard. Although it had never been admitted, his grandparents realised that the pills he had been given from a very young age must have damaged his developing brain. He was retarded and nothing could change that. In consequence, his behaviour was that of a boy much younger than his ten years.

They went by car to nearby woods. As soon as the car stopped, Joe opened the door, letting out Poppy. He ran after Poppy, who rushed ahead of them. He asked if he could throw sticks for her and did so continuously, until he exhausted both himself and the dog. His grandparents pointed out the different trees and wild flowers in the woods, but he showed little interest. On the way home, he told them several times how important it was for Poppy that he came on the walk, although the reverse was true. From Joe's beaming face and happy chatter, they concluded that the walk was a success.

Joe was given an early supper before he returned to the Home. As he munched his sandwiches, he told them what a lovely time he'd had and asked when he could come again. Granny looked at her diary and told him. He asked her to be sure to tell John on their return, so that it could be noted in the book. She assured him that she would do so.

Back at the Home, John asked how the visit had gone and Joe's grandparents assured him that it was good. They booked his next visit and hugged him before they left, but it was easy to tell that mentally he'd returned to the institutionalised part of his life, in which they played no part.

During most of the drive home they said nothing, until Joe's grandfather broke the silence by railing against Joe's unfit mother, who he blamed for Joe being in an institution. His wife gently touched his arm,

"We can't change what has happened," she said. "All we can do is giving him some good moments and happy memories. What I cherish about him is his ready smile and how easy it is to make him happy. I worry too about what will become of him, but that is out of our control. We have to continue helping him in the only way we can."

25
CONVERSATION WITH THE DEAD
By Jake Corey

The dead were his business and Bradley Maudlin enjoyed it. There was as much beauty in the dead as there was revulsion in those alive. The dead were his customers, reliable, predictable. The survivors sickened him, with their blubbing and breaking down in public.

Whilst the atmosphere inside the 'funerarium', as he called it, gave customers an impression of restrained serenity, outside, the wind bent a tree double and rain lashed the hearse pulling up to the loading bay. The violence outside threatened to invade his inner superficial calm. Two pallbearers struggled to lift the coffin, and the brewing storm and the evening gloom fought against them to mark its disapproval. Maudlin glimpsed himself in the window and a moment of nausea struck him, he turned away until he was sure he would not see his own reflection. Satisfied, he turned back and stared through the window, tapping the ashtray with his cigar then removing a fleck of tobacco from his lip.

The sound of the pendulum of the centuries old clock pillaged his silence. There was an urge to smash the object of his loathing but he resisted it, just. The wind battered the pallbearers' jackets, taking a cap and dropping it into a puddle. Maudlin saw the owner's lips move, imagined the man's blasphemy and grimaced. Unnecessary, he thought.

A few minutes later he heard them slide the coffin onto the wooden slab behind him, then silence. They'd wait, he'd be there most of the night, working. The storm would keep him company.

"Unscrew the lid, but leave it on, then leave," he added as an afterthought, "please."

The screws made a complaining squeak, but he didn't turn to watch the process of unscrewing them. The screech of the twisting screws was as if something or someone was pushing against the lid, the screws barely able to restrain it.

A return to silence told him they'd freed the lid. The feel of the men's stares was like a knot in his back. Despite the discomfort, he waited. The contents of the coffin entered his nostrils and he breathed in, sampling the air. There was no greater service, no greater pleasure than to serve those who had reached that state of being he loved. Living for his work was part of him, and this night's work would be special.

Maudlin tapped the ashtray with his cigar and deposited another inch long piece of ash then turned to face the two men. His left arm propped up his right, his cigar close to his lips.

"What is it?" he asked.

"We were told to...," muttered one of the men. The man screwed his cap in his fists and cast his eyes down, water dripped from the cap. The lack of understanding between him and the living was mutual. Maudlin had no wish to understand the living and was indifferent to the livings' opinion of him. Although, he accepted that coming into contact with people was necessary, in general he found the living disagreeable.

"What?" he said,

"They told us to stay...," said the other man and

wiggled a wavering finger at the coffin.

"Go."

As he turned back to the window, he heard the door close with barely a sound. As the last pallbearer's car left the parking area, he deposited his cigar in the ashtray, pulled the curtains and strolled over to the coffin.

Normally, he relished this part of his profession; the cleaning, preparing and the presentational aspects, but this was different, his customer was a friend. Alice had been his only living friend. Almost reverentially, he removed the lid placing it on the floor then he looked into the coffin.

"I never wanted it to end like this," he muttered.

With finger and thumb he picked at the shroud and dropped that too on the floor. Despite his liking for the dead, seeing his friend like this caused him to sag. She was his only friend, now she was dead, but that was the way it had to be.

Maudlin placed a bowl of warm water on the bench then wiped a wet cloth across Alice's wounds, clearing away the clotted blood from her forehead. Try as he might, he couldn't sob. Nothing.

"You silly, foolhardy, ridiculous, beautiful, girl. What have you done?"

Starting at her feet, he'd clean every part of her. He sensed her innocence, knowing so little about her. She was a mystery. But he'd know her more intimately after this night's work than in all the time he'd known her alive.

Hooded eyes hid the lifeless stare of his absurdly forgiving friend. Maudlin pulled up a chair next to the coffin, sat and took her hands in his with a gentleness that the pallbearers would have found impossible to understand of him. He caressed her bare fingers.

"Thank you for giving me a glimpse of your world. Only you have ever seen through me and never gave up. I never thought it would be me who attended to you."

Embarrassment or guilt caused him to shuffle. These feelings were new. No surprise, but they occupied his curiosity. He wasn't one for musing and dwelling because in the long run, it destroyed. Still, she'd been an angel in a world of living demons.

"I wrote you a poem, a bit of doggerel I suppose. I think you'd smile."

A self-conscious chuckle escaped him. He placed both hands over hers and looked at her expressionless face. The softness in his voice surprised him.

"I threw stones at your waves, you caught them and caused not a ripple.

I walked in the rain, you dried my feet.

I gave you vinegar, you sweetened it with honey.

You calmed my demons with your cool breeze.

You opened your door when I wanted only darkness.

You gave me your fluttering eyes and your lilting voice, but I hesitated.

The thread you wove around us, I ripped apart and didn't cry.

You showed the value of living but in the end, the dead don't cry,

Now I'm not strong enough to let you go."

He prided himself that he could look the dead in the eye without flinching. The moistness in his eyes he put down to staring at her without blinking. Even in death she was his friend.

He gathered his thoughts.

"You had a choice but I had none. Death was necessary, perhaps inevitable. Maybe it stopped me becoming," he hesitated, "different. I didn't enjoy what you forced me to do, but your need was greater than mine. Are you happier dead?"

Maudlin sat unmoving until a silence invaded his thoughts and he realised that the clock had stopped. The clock showed two o'clock in the morning. The clock had never stopped before and his reviled father used to boast about the reliability of the damned thing. After these many years, he should have been thankful for the silence.

Legs taking on the composition of rigor mortis, he stood awkwardly, releasing Alice's hands. A sallow expression crossed his face, he felt useless, heavy, abandoned, a man sinking into a marsh. He'd hoped that the last few hours might exorcise his feeling of wretchedness, but he was wrong. As he walked to the window, he was still wrestling with guilt and failure.

He drew the curtain back and peered through the window. A hard drizzle hammered the yard outside, kicking up ripples and forming pools. The lone sodium vapour lamp cast its yellow incandescence, revealing demons swimming in every puddle and crawling along every wall. He turned away, afraid of what was outside, but even more afraid of his own reflection. Sweat ran down his back and tightness in his throat threatened to choke him. He ran his hand across his sweat covered face and clutched at his throat. Unable to move, he was in a nightmare, where death was imminent and he was powerless to stop it. The death he knew was a friend, but this was no friend, this was malevolent.

Maudlin pulled himself together. Regardless of his betrayal, there were only friends in his 'funerarium'. On unsteady legs, he headed towards his study. He needed time to think and he thought better when indulging in his second love, whiskey and cigars, and sensed that this might not be the end of his ordeal.

Entering the study, he hurried to close the curtains then poured himself a drink with shaking hands. Shoulders sagged with relief as he downed the glass of scotch. He poured another almost to the top then reached for his cigar case.

"Bradley, why do you need a drink?" asked a voice behind him.

For the second time that evening, his throat constricted. His head spun towards the voice, his legs failed him and he fell backwards over the drinks trolley as he tried to scramble away from the voice. That malevolence again.

Words struggled to free themselves, like dragging an open umbrella through a thin pipe the wrong way. "What? Who are you?"

"Who I am, isn't important, what I am, is. Think of me as a negotiator," he said in an archaic BBC accent, emphasising the last word.

Maudlin saw the stranger smile then take a sip of his scotch. At least he was human.

"Who are you? How did you get in here? What do you want?"

"I'm not here to hurt you. I'm here to help. To talk with you. To secure your cooperation, if possible," said the man sitting relaxed in the armchair, legs crossed as if he was at home.

Maudlin struggled to his feet, the drinks forgotten amidst the broken glass. There was a standard lamp next to the man, which cast shadows, and he had difficulty focussing on his eyes. In all other respects, the man was as ordinary as any man dressed in a 1950s double-breasted suit could be ordinary. Although recognition evaded him, this man conjured up all his fears and phobias. Here sat the oversized spider in the corner, the torturer with pliers and the hangman's noose.

"Get out now, else I'll call the police," he said, his soprano voice betraying him. Maudlin glanced towards the poker in the fireplace.

The man chuckled. "Come now, don't be so melodramatic. Why don't you get yourself a drink, you need one. Then come, sit and talk. Let's start, we have so much to discuss. Let me explain."

Maudlin thought a drink wasn't such a bad idea. At least he might have a chance of overpowering the man if he could calm his nerves. He picked up the whiskey bottle from the floor where most of the contents had soaked into the carpet. The man patted the other armchair next to him as an elderly uncle might invite his nephew for a cosy chat.

"Tell me what you want," asked Maudlin, not looking at the man. "I'm not used to…"

"The living? Yes, I know. Sometimes the living can be so tiresome and untrustworthy. That's why I'm here. I'm not here to rob you, or kill you, neither am I a deiform on a haunting spree. You have nothing to fear from me, if you cooperate."

Maudlin sat on the edge of the armchair and sipped his scotch, his eyes darted towards the man sitting, relaxed, next to him. They sat in silence for more than a minute before the man seemed satisfied that Maudlin had regained his composure.

"The reason I'm here is that I want to make you an offer. I'm a kind of travel guide," he grinned at Maudlin.

"What sort of travel guide?" interrupted Maudlin.

"It is my job to make sure that the newly dead make it safely to their final destination. Usually, they're happy to be guided, and I'm their guide," said the man as if he was making casual conversation then sipped his scotch.

Maudlin tried to talk, but it came out as a gargle. "Jes… You…"

Warm urine trickled along his crotch and into the chair.

"Some call me 'The Ferryman', such a charming and harmless name, don't you think? Other names aren't perhaps so generous."

"I had to do it. I had no choice. It was for her own good. I explained that to her," said Maudlin, the words falling over themselves, his vocal cords straining to emphasise the words.

"There, there, Bradley. I haven't come for you. Not yet," said the Ferryman.

The Ferryman reached over and patted Maudlin's leg.

"I know that you killed Alice and I know why. Such a noble act." He wagged his finger at Maudlin. "Alice is sought after, a prized commodity. On the one hand, I can deliver her to what you might call perdition, such an unpleasant place. Were you to accept my generous offer, then I might arrange an entirely different, and not altogether unpleasant, eternity. Whether I turn left, or right, perdition or rapture, depends on whether you are prepared to pay the price."

"What is the price?"

"The price of eternal bliss does not come cheap."

The Ferryman's grin would have frozen a blacksmith's forge. "The price? I have performed my role as the Ferryman for an eternity. Since man worked the earth, I have been the Ferryman. I have guided every dead soul to what was in my opinion, their correct destiny. But eternity is unforgiving and I cannot resign my post but the time is approaching when I must move on," his grin broadened, "You have an affinity with the dead, you enjoy their company. If you accept my price, when the time comes, you will be my trainee and in time, I will move on to other things. You will be the new Ferryman. In return, I will look favourably on Alice. It is your decision, but if you agree, we will meet again when your time comes."

A movement in Maudlin's peripheral vision caught his attention. He glanced towards the mirror above the fireplace and saw the barest outline of ... something. He squinted at it as if it was a century's old etching scratched on smoky parchment cast in a fading light. There were only two of them in the room, and neither of them could have cast that image. The shrouded image was the silhouette of Alice, and he understood.

For the first time Maudlin's look fixed the Ferryman's eyes. The Ferryman's stare was so sharp its edge could have cut a hair, but Maudlin stared right back like a condemned man staring down his jailer. "Let us discuss this and I will make my decision," said Maudlin.

Until the light crept under the curtain, the two men talked of innocence and guilt, of loyalty and duty, the dead and one's duty to them. The two discussed higher moral values and amorality, like old companions, if not friends. The Ferryman talked of souls and the soulless. Maudlin spoke of Alice's inner beauty and her flaws and forgiving nature. The Ferryman told Maudlin about the tranquillity of eternal bliss compared to the permanent degeneracy of perdition The Ferryman answered Maudlin's questions with patience and empathy. Occasionally, Maudlin glanced in the mirror and each time the apparition was clearer, until finally he decided. He knew what he had to do.

"So Bradley, it's your choice," the Ferryman said.

Maudlin locked eyes with the Ferryman, who from his expression seemed satisfied with his night's work.

"Ferryman, or Charon as some call you, I rather enjoyed our discussion and I appreciate your candour. You are right, we aren't so different. Loyalty to the dead is for me more important than loyalty to the living. I willingly relinquish my soul and a great deal more for Alice for she is the only living person who has showed me love. Yes, I agree to be your trainee and to become the new Ferryman. Now, please leave."

The Ferryman's face broke into a smile, he stood, walked across to the window with his back to Maudlin. Maudlin sensed that even for a soul not of this world, the Ferryman was happy.

"That is a wise choice, Mr Maudlin, and I look forward to enjoying a longer discussion with you, under different circumstances," his smile brought no comfort to Maudlin.

"I have confidence in you as my replacement, and as for eternity, your demise is only a heartbeat away, so enjoy the time you have remaining."

The Ferryman paused, seeming to have a final thought. "The poetry, Mr Maudlin?"

"Yes?"

"Don't give up the funeral business, you are no Dylan Thomas. Good morning to you."

The Ferryman left the room, not floating through a wall, but as a mortal, by the door. Maudlin sagged in his armchair, blew out his breath, and as an afterthought, downed the remains of his scotch. With steady hands, he smoked his cigar and sat in contemplation. Walking over and looking around the curtains, he saw that there was no storm, no rain. There was billowing clouds and air so clear that for the first time the oak tree his father had planted fifty years ago was spectacular. It must have been after seven o'clock in the morning and he needed to prepare for the day.

Maudlin walked through to the 'funerarium' to where the body of Alice lay. He stared down at the woman who, in life, might have made so much of a difference in his life. Now in death, she would transform him.

Her body seemed to be as he'd left it, but as he looked closer, his eyebrows narrowed. Alice's eyes were still closed, but she was smiling. The eternity ring he'd given her months ago was now on her finger.

For the first time, Bradley Maudlin returned her smile.

26
DO AS YOU WOULD BE DONE BY
By Linda Nash

Georgette seized the canopy designed to cover her market stall and dropped the pole that she was attempting to insert into one of the corners. Her nervousness was making her clumsy. This was her first visit as a stall holder at Lorgnon Market, where she intended to sell eggs, butter and vegetables from their smallholding in Bledy. Her husband, Jacques, had driven Georgette the ten kilometres to the market in the horse and trap, and had left her to go over to the cattle market where he hoped to buy two more milking cows. Lost in thought, she did not hear at first, a woman's voice asking her something.

"I'm sorry, what did you say?" she said, coming back to earth with a start. Looking up, she saw a pretty dark haired woman smiling at her.

"I wondered if I could be of any help. By the way, my name is Esther."

"Oh please," said Georgette, "this is my first time at the market, and I feel rather nervous, which doesn't help my practical skills, which at the best of times aren't wonderful."

While Esther helped her to place the cover over her

stall, which was nothing more than a large table, Georgette noticed how stylishly she dressed. She particularly liked her brown felt hat on which was pinned a yellow butterfly brooch.

"I hope you don't mind me saying so, but what a beautiful hat."

"Oh, do you like it?" said Esther looking pleased. "Actually, that's what I sell here - hats," and she pointed to her stall, which was a little further on. It was piled high with hats in various colours, shapes and sizes.

"I make hats in my spare time," she said. "I live in Brussels. Where do you live?"

"I live about ten kilometres from here on the edge of Bledy. My husband and I have a small holding."

Georgette unpacked her baskets, laying out the packets of butter, goat cheeses and then carefully piled up the eggs. On the other side of the table she arranged bunches of carrots, lettuces, peas and leeks. Now she was ready for when potential customers arrived. She glanced at the church clock, it was almost seven o' clock. The first customers were arriving, so, with luck, they would soon be busy. She realised, looking around her, that she was one of several stalls selling farm produce.

Esther returned to her stall and Georgette decided that if there was a lull she would go and take a closer look at Esther's creations and maybe buy one. Goodness, she couldn't remember the last time she had bought herself a new hat. It would be just the thing to start tongues wagging at Mass on Sunday.

By half past ten Georgette had sold everything on her stall and for the first time in almost three hours she glanced over in Esther's direction. Although, she could see that there were fewer hats on her stall than when she'd set up, there were still several remaining. Quickly packing up her stall, Georgette took the canopy down and folded it with care. She placed it on the table together with the poles, sliding her empty baskets underneath. Then, she walked over to see Esther, who was selling a blue hat with a brim and trimmed with a feather to an unattractive overweight lady with a bright red complexion, whom Georgette recognised as a farmer's wife from Bredy. She was peering into a hand mirror held by Esther.

"I'm not sure it suits me," she said doubtfully.

"Bonjour Clementine, what a lovely hat, such a pretty shade of blue and that feather gives it the finishing touch," said Georgette, tactfully omitting to mention anything about the hat suiting her.

"Then I'll take it," said Clementine reaching for her purse. She counted her change, putting it carefully away in her pocket and went off with her purchase smiling happily.

When she had disappeared, Georgette looked at Esther and they both smiled wryly.

"Thank you, Georgette, I was lost for words, the poor woman had already tried on at least five hats and frankly speaking, none of them suited her."

"Neither did the blue one," said Georgette and they both burst out laughing.

"I'm going to get a cup of coffee from the cafe, would you like one, Esther?"

Georgette came back a few minutes later holding two cups of coffee and handed one to Esther.

"I didn't know how you liked your coffee," she said, handing it to Esther, "so I brought sugar to go with it."

"Perfect," said Esther sipping her coffee gratefully. "How much do I owe you?"

"Nothing, after all if it hadn't been for your help I would still have been erecting my stall."

"Is that your husband," said Esther looking in the direction of Georgette's stall, where a puzzled looking man was looking in every direction except the right one.

"Oh goodness," said Georgette. "I had forgotten about Jacques."

They both laughed again and Georgette walked over to her husband. She exchanged a few words with him. He picked up her empty baskets and went off in the direction of the cafe.

"He's gone to join some pals for a beer or two," said Georgette on returning to Esther's stall, "which gives us at least an hour together. What time is your train back to Brussels?"

"Twelve thirty."

In the hour that remained until the market ended, the two women told each other about their families. Georgette learned that Esther's husband Jacob worked long hours in the leather industry, and that they found it difficult to manage on the little he earned. As Esther had learned dressmaking and tailoring, she had decided to help make ends meet by making hats and selling them at local markets. Her two children, Miriam, 9, and Joseph, 15, attended school in Brussels not far from their home near the North station.

Esther discovered that like her, Georgette had two children, a son, Marcel, 14, and a daughter, Christine, 10. It was difficult too for her family too to make a sufficient living from their smallholding. On it they had ten milking cows, two goats, a couple of dozen hens and a vegetable plot, where there was adequate space to grow enough vegetables for their own consumption and to sell. They had until recently sold their produce locally, but had decided that they should try their luck further afield. They felt that markets would be a good way to earn extra income. Georgette explained that the market at Lorgnon had been a trial run and that she hoped that Vassy market would be a possibility. This was a small town, further away, in the direction of Brussels.

Esther smiled in delight.

"That's wonderful!" I have a stall there, too. It's a busy market and much larger than the one here."

The two women continued to chat until Jacques arrived for Georgette. She introduced him to her new friend. On hearing that Esther's family lived in an apartment in

Brussels, Jacques invited them to come to visit them on a Sunday when they were free.

They said their goodbyes, promising to look out for each other at Vassy market, which was in three days' time on Friday.

On the way home, Georgette thanked her husband for inviting her new friend and her family to visit them.

"I could see you two were getting on like a house on fire and she seemed a nice enough woman. It will make a pleasant change to get to know a family outside Bledy."

Georgette squeezed his arm gratefully. He was a generous man and very much aware of the limitations of their neighbourhood.

"Oh dear," she said, clutching his arm.

"What is it," he said alarmed.

"I was going to buy myself a new hat and we were talking so much I completely forgot."

"Goodness," Jacques said laughing, "I thought something terrible had happened. You will have plenty of time to buy a hat. After all, you will be seeing your new friend again in three days. I think with a name like Esther, your new friend must be Jewish."

"I suppose she must be," said Georgette. "I don't think we know any other Jews, do we?"

When Friday came, Georgette arrived in Vassy a little before 6:30 a.m. to find that Esther had started setting up her stall. They greeted each other like old friends, and Esther said she had spoken to Jacob and that if it suited Jacques and Georgette, they would like to come and visit on Sunday, in just over a week's time.

This they did, and to Georgette and Esther's delight both husbands took to each other, in spite of or perhaps because of their very different backgrounds. The children, too, were soon chatting away and Marcel and Christine took Joseph and Miriam off to the village to introduce them to their friends.

This became the pattern for many weekends, although

Georgette and Jacques and their children also went to Brussels. They marvelled at the Grand Place and the beautiful art deco buildings in nearby streets. Without their new friends they would probably never have visited Brussels, and even if they had, would not have known what to look at without Jacob and Esther's knowledge as city dwellers.

A little under a year later, Jacob and Esther invited them to celebrate the New Year in Brussels.

As the church clock chimed midnight and 1938 became the New Year, they lifted their glasses to their continuing friendship and happiness, but Jacob added a sombre note to their celebrations.

"I have heard that Jews are being badly treated in Germany," he said. "Many have left and those that stay suffer discrimination."

"But, how can that be?" exclaimed Jacques. "After all, during the Great War, both Jews and Gentiles fought side by side, and surely everybody who lives there is considered to be German."

Jacob shook his head sadly.

"You're right they are all German, but in spite of that they're being persecuted. I wish it weren't true, but the stories I have heard come from friends who have relatives there."

"But this could never happen in Belgium," said Georgette. "We're all Belgians, it never occurs to us that people are different, and as for treating them badly, that is quite unthinkable." She put her arm around Esther, who had turned pale.

"Don't worry, Esther, if anything bad happens here, you and your family can come and stay with us and we will protect you."

"Oh, we couldn't possibly take advantage of you and anyway where would you put us?" Esther said, her eyes filling with tears at her friend's generosity.

"We have a saying," replied Georgette. "Do as you

would be done by. If the day comes when you need our help we will welcome you into our home. I am certain that you would be ready to do the same for us."

Esther's cheeks were wet with tears. She hugged Georgette.

"Thank you for your generosity, but I am sure we are safe here in Brussels and will never have to take you up on your kind offer. Let's drink to that shall we? To continued friendship, generosity and love."

27
A STROKE OF LUCK
By Vesla Small

"Heavy rain causes severe disruption to the transport network..."

John heard the weatherman's voice through the crackling of his car radio.

The banks of the rivers had burst due to heavy rainfall, and John drove slowly through the flooded streets, until he no longer dared risk continuing. The village seemed abandoned, like a ghost town. The streets were turning into rivers, and the gardens into lakes. Sandbags were stacked up around houses, and John dreaded the thought of what the interiors would look like, hopefully, its inhabitants had been evacuated. A truck drove past him and nearly 'drowned' his car.

"Bastard!" he roared, and made a mental note of the registration plate, 'DA25367.'

"Bloody foreigner!" he cursed.

His mobile rang. It was his wife. "Yes dear, I'll be as quick as I can."

'Will I be able to make it in time?' he fretted as he struggled to navigate out of the flooded area and up the hill.

When he reached the summit of the hill, John almost hit a middle-aged woman, running towards his car.

The poor woman seemed scared, and yelled, "Quickly! My partner's injured."

John parked the car on the roadside and followed the woman.

"He's behind the crag over there," she said, and pointed towards the moors.

They walked at a fast pace until suddenly she stopped. She crouched, held her hand against her chest and took shallow breaths.

"I feel pain in my chest and need to slow down, but I'll follow you," she apologised.

John continued to run, without giving the woman a second thought.

"Help's here. Where are you?" he called out as he approached the crag.

There was nobody, and when he turned around, he realised the woman was nowhere to be seen.

At first, he worried that her condition was worse than he'd first thought, but then he suspected that something dodgy had happened, and John's first thought was his car.

As he walked back, he became conscious of the rough landscape. The path turned and rose between heather, bushes and rocks, and he was soon out of breath. He stumbled over a tree stump and felt his ankle twist in an awkward position. The pain was terrible. Panicking, he clenched his teeth, 'I need to get back to the road. Eileen needs me.'

Feeling helpless, he shouted, but nobody came to his rescue. He staggered back to the road, wondering if his car was still there. Finally, he reached the road and the place where he'd parked the car and as predicted, the car was gone with his belongings.

"Bloody thief!" his words echoed.

By now the pain was excruciating. He sat on a small

rock at the side of the river, cooling his ankle in the freezing water and after a while, he felt comfort. Desperate for something to support his injured foot, he trod carefully to limit the weight bearing on the injured ankle, heading for a plastic bag he'd spotted on the roadside. His eyes lit up when he realised it contained a scarf and a fleece jacket. 'Something to support my ankle, and to keep me warm,' he thought, as a tired smile crossed his face.

The pain eased after he'd wrapped the scarf tightly from his toes to his mid-calf, but when he walked again, the pain returned. In despair, he pulled out two boundary stakes from the roadside to use as crutches.

The late afternoon air was cool. No matter how much he stared at the deserted road, there was no car in sight. John leaned on the wooden poles and hobbled along the highland road. Tension showed. Tired and hungry, he felt tightness around his forehead, as if his head was in a vice. He stopped and sat on a stone at the side of the road.

A herd of hairy highland cattle munched on hay as they stood inside an open stone shelter, away from the wind, looking curiously at John. He jumped in surprise when a young deer shot out from a copse. The rock ptarmigan cooed and pecked seeds and insects in the open vegetation, undisturbed by his presence. Under normal circumstances, John would have enjoyed the walk across the highlands, if it hadn't been for the stolen car, the injured ankle and the need to get back home.

His ankle felt hot and swollen under the scarf. A couple of cars drove past without stopping. Frustrated and on the point of giving up, John spotted the truck.

'Plate number DA25367,' he thought, with a mixture of anticipation and irritation. 'It's the same truck that nearly 'drowned' my car.'

He walked into the road and gave the chauffeur no option but to stop.

The man rolled down the window, and asked in a loud, cheerful voice, "Need a lift?"

"Yes, please."

After he'd told the driver about his misfortune, John asked, "Can I use your mobile? I need to contact my wife who's in a quandary."

"There's no satellite signal up here," the driver explained. "You can try once we're on the other side of the highland."

It started to rain. There was something soothing and hypnotic in watching the windshield wipers sweeping the water away and whilst listening to the driver speaking, in a deep and pleasant voice, John dozed off.

It was dusk when John opened his eyes and tried to figure out the time on his watch in the light of the lit up control panel. The music from the loudspeakers, and the flashing lights from the dashboard, reminded him more of a discotheque than a truck cabin.

"I'm singing in the rain...," the driver sounded cheerful, lifted his shoulders to relieve the tension, and winked to John. "We'll soon be there. You'll be like new and ready for action after that snooze."

The truck moved at a snail's pace along the road. When they stopped outside John's house, Rita, his mother-in-law waited outside.

"Hurry John," she said, "Eileen's in labour. We need a doctor or a nurse."

This was their first child and John felt helpless. With an injured leg, he could not help his wife, during the most important moment in their married life.

The truck driver sensed his predicament, got out of the truck and walked towards Rita.

"I worked as a midwife before deciding on a change of career. If you don't mind, I'll be pleased to help. Bring me clean clothes. Prepare hot water and clean towels... and scissors," he added in a firm, but kind tone of voice, as he unbuttoned and removed his oil stained coveralls.

Rita listened, nodded, and led them into the house.

John limped over to Eileen, who was lying in bed.

Tears came to his eyes.

"There at last," she said, reached for his hand, and smiled with her teeth clenched together.

"Another push will do."

John heard the truck driver's words, followed by the baby's first cry. John looked at his wife, with joy and relief.

Moonlight spilled into the room and a healthy baby boy was placed on Eileen's chest. They named him Bjørn for 'Bear' after the Scandinavian truck driver.

28
A SUMMER ROMANCE
By Jake Corey

My wife and I are heading off to Gaborone on holiday. This is not a normal holiday, but a get away from 'Her' holiday. My wife knows of 'Her' and she's cool about 'Her'. We walk towards Passport Control and there 'She' is on the right, near the newspaper stand, a seductive vixen temptress, looking at me and flashing herself. 'She's' stalking me you know. 'She' wouldn't let me go, even if I wanted to, and I don't. I want it to go on forever. I'm weak and my wife understands, she pulls me away, more in encouragement than chastisement. I'm silly, according to my wife. But my infatuation is consuming, she doesn't understand the strength of our relationship. It's real. I can't get away from 'Her'. I'm afraid that if we don't leave here soon I might do something bad. 'She' looks my way as we pass.

Some weeks ago my wife asked me how long it's been going on. That's the first question wives ask, isn't it? I told her 'months' but I lied. It's more like years, long erotic, sensual, tiring wonderful years. At first it was good, not great but 'good'. It got better over time and I became obsessed with 'Her'. Now, I can't do without 'Her'. 'She's' there when I go to sleep and when I wake. I'm possessed. How wicked does that sound? Yes, I know it sounds dreadful. I've spent a fortune on 'Her' as well, which makes it doubly distressing. But I can't help it. My goodness, 'She' was so subtle, so seductive. Dressed in red, gold, blue or silver, 'She's' delightful and even better when 'She's' undressed. 'Her' appearance, 'Her' smell, 'Her' taste. I'd kill for 'Her'.

We pass through Passport Control. The official asks us why we're going to Gaborone. I'm speechless, looking back, over my shoulder, "That's the only way we can get away from 'Her'," my wife answers enigmatically. "It's the only place where 'She' can't follow."

The official scowls, he's heard it before. "Yeah, whatever," he replies with rolling eyes.

We hurry through 'Security' and for a moment, we're free of 'Her'. Is 'She' behind us or in front? It's hard to tell. My wife watches me as I empty my bag onto the conveyor belt, to be sure I'm not taking one of 'Her' 'souvenirs' with me. A little red thing drops out of my pocket. My wife chastises me with a stare, takes 'Her' between finger and thumb, and slips it into her own handbag, which closes with a satisfying 'click'.

Hurrying through towards Gate 43, I breathe a sigh of relief and wipe my sweaty face with my handkerchief. My God, there 'She' is outside 'Leaders', looking my way. 'She's' exposing more than 'She' should, and I head off in her direction, smiling. 'She's' won. My wife of fifteen years is left behind, forgotten in a heartbeat. 'She' flashes those red lips and I can smell 'Her' from here.

I cry out, "Yes, yes, I'll come with you. If only to taste the fruits of your loins one more time. darling."

My wife sees me and her look says it all. She's used to this and knows what 'She's' like. 'She's' the worst there's been, and there's been a few. People are staring at us as my wife pulls on my jacket sleeve and takes me away from 'Her'.

"Come on dear. This will not do. Try harder. Gate 43 is a few minutes' walk and then you'll be free. I can have you to myself and 'She' can go to hell," she says, hurrying.

My wife hurries me along, as I look over my shoulder at 'Her'. She's not following and a part of me is thankful. This romance would test the resolve of any man, even a eunuch. 'She' is the ultimate temptress and I realise I'm whimpering, blubbering. What am I going to do for a full month without seeing 'Her'? I won't sleep, I'll pine, I'll die of wanton loneliness.

We board the plane to Gaborone Botswana, population a quarter of a million. My wife has assured me, 'She' can't follow us there. I hope she's wrong. No! I mean right, for my own sanity. And when I return to Belgium, it's possible the love and romantic affair will have faded.

The plane reaches cruising height and the Stewardess walks the aisle. Looking down at me, she asks if we need anything. I whimper with frustration, 'yes, I need 'Her',' is on my lips. My wife pats my sleeve and tells me to take a tablet, sleep and I'll feel better.

Before I fade into oblivion, I try to concentrate on Botswana. It's considered to be the least corrupt country in Africa and ranks close to Portugal and South Korea. Interesting, but not enough to take my mind away from 'Her'. My eyes blur and as they start to droop I see another man with 'Her'. Damn it, he's brought 'Her' with him. They appear so happy together. He brings 'Her' lips to his and there is the briefest kiss. He has 'Her' scent, only 'She' has a distinctive scent. The temptress, 'She' should be mine. I almost stand and make a scene with the man, demand to know what 'She's' doing on the plane and what is he doing with 'Her'? I'm not selfish though, I love 'Her' so much, I'm even prepared to share 'Her'. You seductress, you wanton hussy… you…you Lady Godiva!

My eyes droop and I fade into sleep, thankful sleep. I haven't slept properly for weeks, thinking of 'Her', my little Belgian mistress. A whole month without seeing her.

I feel as if my heart will break but I know my memory of 'Her' will fade with time. But for the moment, my love for 'Her' is so strong, so painful... so 'here and now'. I yearn to see 'Her' once more and taste 'Her' lips. As I drift off, I know that any man who's been 'In Love' will know what I'm dreaming of. It's the same dream I have every night.

It starts with the rapturous feel of unwrapping a bar of Belgian chocolate. The heavenly texture and her taste. Then comes that first taste of Côte d'Or or Corné Port Royal. The texture, the sweetness on my tongue, sliding along the grooves of the pieces of heaven and finally, the melting nectar slipping down my throat.

29
USE YOUR GUMPTION
By Vesla Small

In all the years before the war, the clock had never stopped.

It was 27 May 1940, following the bombing by the Luftwaffe, which had levelled the city of Bodø, almost half the population was homeless. The German soldiers were now ransacking the few remaining houses, in search of potential housing for their troops.

***

"Kommen Sie mit!" the German soldier's steel blue eyes gazed at the man facing him.

Nils Grube was preparing dinner with his fiancée when the German soldiers stormed into the kitchen.

"Why? What do you want from me?" he sounded shocked.

"We found a weapon in your outhouse. You hid it. It's a Lee Enfield rifle .303, a weapon used by the British military," the soldier frowned and showed Nils the rifle.

For the last couple of days, the German soldiers had searched high and low in the hayloft and the stables. They left the outhouse until last, where the English soldiers had stayed.

"No, you're wrong. The English soldier staying in the pigeon house must have left the rifle. They left in a rush when you arrived. It's not mine!" Nils sounded adamant.

His fiancée, Anna Martens, stood by his side, and listened.

"Nein, kommen Sie mit!" the young soldier sounded unyielding, and looked at the couple without pity. "Sofort!"

Two soldiers grasped Nils by his arms.

Anna rushed towards the door and blocked it with her body.

"You can't take him away. He's innocent. He's done nothing wrong," she protested.

"Herr Grube must come for interrogation. Now! To the police station!" the soldier said, pushing her aside.

But Anna stood there like a rock, fearless. She embraced her fiancé and whispered, "I'll do everything to get you back, I promise."

She watched her fiancé leave with the soldiers, and saw he looked hunched over, tired and disillusioned.

The bombing of Bodø had been a horrific experience for all of them. Anna recalled the day when she and Nils had been on their bicycles, in the middle of it, trying to escape from the Luftwaffe. The enemy had destroyed the city with their bombs. This was too much.

As the German military staff car disappeared, she grabbed her gabardine coat, put on a hat and slipped her feet into a pair of galoshes. The brisk walk cleared her head. Anna made a long distance call to her parents and told them of the distressing incident.

"Use your gumption," her father advised her.

Anna knew that living so far apart troubled her father, especially when the war started, in April that year.

How on earth could she use her common sense? Everybody knew about the Gestapo and their threats. She held her emotions in check until she reached the house, then she fell apart, and wept herself to sleep.

The next morning, Anna thought about what her father had said, "Use your gumption."

After she'd met her boss and informed her colleagues about what had happened, she headed for the Gestapo's temporary headquarters. The first thing she spotted on the wall behind the German soldier was the swastika flag. She viewed the swastika with contempt, and a shiver of fear went down her spine.

"Bitte?" the young soldier was courteous, but uncompromising.

'Judging by his manners, he must come from a good German family, but so young, and so far away from his Vaterland,' she thought.

"I've come to see Mister Nils Grube, brought here last night for investigation," she said, measuring her words.

"Name please?" the soldier asked.

"I'm Anna Martens, and Nils Grube is my fiancé," she replied.

The soldier examined her identity card, nodded and escorted Anna along the corridor. As she hurried behind him, she noticed that his posture had an air of blatant authority, that of a typical SS soldier. He stopped outside a door, knocked and opened it for her.

"Guten Tag. I'm Major Kurz," the uniformed man sounded friendly, he stood up from behind his desk and shook Anna's hand.

Major Kurz was a middle aged man, with a chiselled face, and a slightly overhanging stomach under the smart uniform. Next to him sat a Gestapo officer, the interpreter. The small, narrow mouth made him look unfriendly.

"What can I do for you?" the Major asked Anna and offered her a chair.

Anna explained that she'd come to learn news of her fiancé and wanted to know if there was anything she could do to help.

The Major told her that there was nothing she could do, and that she had to wait out the time it took to deal with the case. He reminded her that Mister Grube was accused of hiding a weapon, a serious offence, and time was needed to examine the situation. In the meantime, he would be kept in a prison cell.

"I'd like to visit him, if I can," Anna looked at him, determination showing in her eyes.

"I'm afraid he may be transferred to Trondhjem Kretsfengsel. Come back tomorrow and I'll arrange a visit," Major Kurz sounded caring, and put his hand on her shoulder.

"Trondhjem prison?" Anna gasped and stared at the Major. "No, that can't be!"

"I'm afraid so," the Major responded. "If worse comes to worse, it'll be Grini prison in Oslo, next. It depends on the outcome," he looked troubled by Anna's distressed stare.

"You can't punish an innocent man," she protested.

"The Gestapo can be dangerous if you cross them. It's no laughing matter," Major Kurz bit his bottom lip, and drew his eyebrows together.

The Major's words frightened Anna.

"I'm sorry, Fraülein."

Although concerned about her fiancé's future, she pulled herself together, shook the Major's hand, forced her lips into a smile, and said, "Thank you for your time. I'll be back tomorrow."

On her way back home, Anna felt she might have an ally in Major Kurz, who seemed to be a good listener and to give helpful advice. She would do her utmost to nurture friendship between them, and to follow her father's advice, to use her gumption. Walking home, through the bombed streets, there was a spring in her step. The sun was shining and soon it would be midnight, the sun would show above the horizon and illuminate the Landego Island with its warming and wonderful light and colours. Anna felt hopeful and energetic.

***

The next day, Anna left the house in high spirits, on her way to visit Nils. She baked a loaf of bread and packed cheese, margarine and jam in a paper bag. Aware of how important it was for Nils to have a well shaved face, she added shaving cream.

Her hair blew in the wind, as she strode through the bombed roads, her shoulders back and face held high. Anna looked at her best for her fiancé, not knowing when they'd meet again.

As she entered the prison cell, she saw that Nils couldn't keep his eyes off her. She walked towards him with poise and smiled. Returning her smile, he stood, stretched out his arms, and hugged her.

"How did the interrogation go? Were you able to prove your innocence?" Anna whispered as she released him from the embrace.

"No, not yet," he sounded apologetic.

Anna looked at him, and thought, 'I've always admired his long straight nose and his air of wisdom, and I wasn't wrong about that. He's the wisest and kindest man I've ever known. He's the perfect man for me.'

"Do you have a weakness we can use to your advantage?" Anna was surprised after she'd said it.

"Hmm, possibly," his voice was breaking. "When I was twelve years old, I suffered from gangrene, and they amputated my left foot. Twenty years later, I suffered from spinal tuberculosis and they treated me in a sanatorium. Maybe that will make them think?"

Nils appeared to regain control of his voice, sounding more optimistic.

"It was when I returned home from the sanatorium I purchased the chiming clock on the wall," he laughed, and winked at Anna.

"Yes, of course," Anna said, and smiled back. "I love the deep, warm chiming sound the clock makes. I'll be waiting for you to wind it up on your return."

They sat quietly, one on each side of the table, held each other's hands for a while, until a Norwegian prison guard called out, "You must leave now."

Anna embraced Nils, "I'll ask for a meeting with Major Kurz as soon as possible. Be good! Remember, I'll keep my promise," Anna said, embraced Nils, and left the room, all the time with her fiancé on her mind.

***

Two days later, Anna returned to Major Kurz's office. To her surprise, she learnt he was a medical doctor. While they talked, she could hear Grieg's 'Morning Mood'. The sound of the soothing music uplifted her and gave her hope.

Major Kurz looked at Anna, and smiled, "Edvard Grieg composed wonderful music. He's my favourite composer."

After Anna had described Nils's medical history, the Major scratched his head with bewilderment.

"Fraülein Martens, this reinforces my belief that the Gestapo may consider releasing him from prison. They cannot afford to take risks if we claim he's infected with tuberculosis. I'll examine him and make recommendations to that effect," Major Kurz sounded determined. "I'll do my best to promote his case. Come back in one week."

***

When Anna came back to see Wolfgang Kurz the following week, he sounded less optimistic. "Sorry, Fraülein Martens, I recommended that the Gestapo discharge Herr Grube but to no avail. But let's not give in."

By the sound of it, Major Kurz did not intend to give up the fight, nor did Anna.

When transferred to Trondhjem County Prison, two weeks later, there was a spark of hope in Nils's heart, confident that Anna would do everything to reunite them.

Wolfgang Kurz looked as if he admired Anna for her courage and perseverance. Neither of them gave up. Justice prevailed and after three months, Anna and Nils were reunited.

This man, Wolfgang Kurz, represented the enemy, there was no question, but as a person, at a human level, Anna liked him.

***

The first thing Nils did, when he came back home, was to rewind the clock on the wall which hadn't been wound up since that day when the Gestapo took him away.

And in years to come, every Friday, before Nils went to bed, Anna would watch her husband wind up the clock, a delicate operation, requiring a steady hand and careful attention.

On the night of his death, the clock stopped. Although, it's still hanging in the same place, nobody has been able to make it work. No one was sure why.

30
THE PRINCE AND I
By Jake Corey

He was in a huff; more than huff; he was in a fudgy as his mother called it. The Prince was unhappy. Sitting in the plane with his hands in his lap, his lower lip protruded. He'd refused drinks and eats. It was his way of telling those around him and that meant everyone, that the Prince was not amused.

Whilst preparing for the trip, his mother had sent him a note. He suspected the Chief Secretary to Her Majesty had advised her of its necessity. It had read:

'During your trip to Dubai, you are requested and required by Her Majesty, to acquit yourself such as to avoid bringing Her Majesty or the Royal Household into disrepute. You are requested and required to refrain from making official statements, or of entering into agreements, official or otherwise.'

He was royal, for heaven's sake, although not first in line to the throne. In his opinion, he had more intelligence than his older brother, and he'd told him so. The Prince had a Sociology degree from Oxford and that had been jolly hard, especially when one had to attend to royal business to boot. No one else in his family had to work as hard as him, for sure. Still, he knew he must stop this self-indulgence. He wanted to give the public an image of himself as a 'doer', a practical, man of the people, not a 'Lotus Eater'.

As a stewardess walked by, he said, "Get me Patrick."

"We'll be landing in a few minutes, sir," her smile never slipping.

"Get him," he said.

The British Airways stewardess smiled down at him, turned around the way she'd come and hurried away. He looked back and admired her sashay. Patrick, his protection person, or aid, as he liked to consider him, was the only person allowed to accompany him on unofficial trips. Patrick travelled in Second Class, it was the tax payer's money after all. The Royal Protection Officer stood over the Prince then down onto his haunches.

"Yes, Sir. What can I do for you?"

"Patrick, old chap, they know we're coming, don't they? Will they have a car for us?"

"They do. Bit tricky getting a car though. But we got one, from the Embassy. A Consular Official will meet us. Seems they get royals visiting every two minutes, and yours is a private visit."

Patrick could be blunt and Prince Albert liked that. Patrick meant to say, 'Minor Royals in Dubai are two a penny, and they'd send a clerk and a taxi to meet them.' So he'd get no red carpet; what a let down. His thoughts were still mulling over the indignity of it when Patrick's voice broke in.

"..landing in a few minutes."

"We're staying at the Burj place. Right?" asked the Prince.

"'Burj Al Arab', that's right, a suite. Not on the top floor, but I understand it's ok," Patrick pronounced suite, 'suit' and the Prince smiled.

"Races, when's the races, Patrick?"

"Tomorrow. You don't need me, do you? Thought I might do the bazaars; if that's ok with you. Someone from the Dubai Royal family's hosting you, I understand."

The stewardess approached and spoke to Patrick, "Sir, we're landing now. Please take your seat."

The Prince sensed that she'd aimed the rebuke at him and he pouted.

He interjected, "I'm talking. A moment. Tell the pilot to go slower, there's a good girl."

The Prince smiled at her, convinced she was overwhelmed by his presence and charm.

Turning to Patrick, he said, "Yes, ok. Take the day off tomorrow. You'd better sit, old chap, otherwise there'll be a letter to the palace, complaining," said the Prince, rolling his eyes.

The plane circled over Dubai and he saw the The Burj Khalifa, tallest building in the world. No doubt someone would suggest that he visit it. Life could be so tiresome, demands, demands, demands, always, demands. He wanted to get away from his frightful family, visit the races, have a little fun. Not much to ask, especially on a private visit. No publicity, no speeches and there'd be no recording of his every movement. Quite right too, after all, his mother was paying for the trip,

The plane landed at Dubai International Airport in the heat of the morning sun. After a seven-hour flight, he was as stiff as a prisoner in the Tower of London, and in need of care and attention. At least he was first to disembark from the plane. The lack of ceremony surprised him. Even he had to produce his passport. Patrick tried to placate the Arab policeman who'd made the demand, to be told to get in line. Didn't they know of his arrival? He was royal, for pity's sake. He'd have something to say to the Ambassador.

It seemed to the Prince that the Consul was in a hurry to drop the Prince off at the Burj Al Arab Hotel. To the Prince, that was 'not on' and he looked at the Consul in such a way that four hundred years ago, he'd have arranged the man's removal from office, or worse. Prince Albert sighed, 'What had times come to?'

The Prince waited at the entrance to the hotel and Patrick followed with the Prince's carry-on bag. The doorman seemed indifferent to Prince Albert, second son of the Queen of the United Kingdom of Great Britain and Northern Ireland. He was unmoved that the Prince was waiting outside a hotel. It's a hotel for heaven's sake.

The doorman said something to the Prince, who ignored him. Patrick came to the rescue and spoke to the Arab in the traditional English way.

"This is Prince Albert. Let him in," Patrick explained, like an Englishman talking to Johnny foreigner, bending to the doorman's level, he stared at him, eyes bulging, Marty Feldman style. The doorman remained unconcerned, and the Prince thought he'd heard the impudent chap say 'credit card'.

Patrick turned to the Prince with a look that may have been anger or apology, he could never be sure with Patrick.

"Sir, the chap says you need to swipe your credit card in the slide there," he said pointing to a mechanism with a slot. "It checks to see if you're good for the bill."

"Good for the bill?" he said, his eyes coming to the boil. "Bloody impudent pipsqueak. I'll have words with His Royal Highness about this. I can tell you."

The Prince produced his wallet and extracted a Diners Club card, which he handed to Patrick, looking away as if it disturbed his royal presence.

"May I help you?" the voice from behind said, in impeccable English. It quite took the Prince by surprise.

The Prince turned and saw a femme fatale; a cross between Venus and Princess Diana. Sunglasses on head, Gucci bag over her shoulder and slacks so tight, Stephen Hawking would have had difficulty slipping an atom down there. The woman smiled at the Prince; a smile capable of melting the arctic icecap faster than global warming, and offered him her hand. She offered no normal hand but the hand of a sempiternal goddess. She was the 'Three Graces' corporeal, and so tall he had to look up to see into her soul. Her titian hair flowed like a river toward every Prince's dream and her blue eyes might have seared through Superman.

"I am Princess Astrid Bint Ali, the daughter of the Crown Prince. I'm staying here, is there a problem?"

"Charmed," said Prince Albert, lingering over the offered hand, which he considered brushing with his lips but resisted the temptation. "I'm Prince Albert. Son of the Queen,"

"Silly, which queen?" she asked, smiling into his eyes. "We get so many here I lose count."

"Queen of England. Sorry."

The Princess laughed and extracted her hand, putting it to her mouth as her smile widened. "I know that, you nana. I'm joking. Pleased to meet you."

Turning to the doorman, she spoke in rapid Arabic. In the time it took Prince Albert to pocket his Diners Club card, her face changed from the Goddess of Grace to the Goddess of Wrath.

"Follow me. When I'm in Dubai, I stay here. I'm on the top floor," she said, in a matter of fact way.

The doorman operated a remote control and double, gold and glass doors swung inwards, as the doorman bowed as low as he could without getting to his knees. The Prince thought better of the man for recognising his obvious royal pedigree.

"Gosh, that's terif'. How did you get that?" he asked, still smiling.

"My father owns it. Do you play tennis?" she asked, turning towards the Prince, her charm now returned.

"Rather. I've had a knock about with Andy Murray. But I haven't brought my racket," he said, swishing an air racket backwards and forwards.

"Never mind; meet me on the roof in half an hour."

31
THE TRUTH BEHIND THE MYTH
By Vesla Small

"Darling, we've received an invitation to the Royal Garden Party!" Abbey was excited. "Jason, imagine strolling in the garden, cakes, tea, celebrities, royalty."

Her husband smiled and looked at his wife, with whom he'd been married for five years, to the surprise of his family and friends. With a career as a lawyer, he'd had little time for the opposite sex, so he'd had no desire to settle down and start a family. He was forty, and she was twenty, when they'd met at the university where he'd been a replacement lecturer, and she was one of the students. Charmed by her spontaneity, curiosity and thirst for knowledge, she'd conquered his heart from the moment he set his eyes on her.

Abbey knew that she had her husband in her palm, since the day her father told his son-in-law he'd named his daughter Abbey, 'the joy of the father'. Jason had responded with a laugh, "She's my joy now."

"I'll wear the blue studded dress with short sleeves and the blue fascinator with a netted veil. The peep toe heels, I bought on eBay, will be just the thing. And short gloves will finish my outfit nicely," she went on and on, with passion.

"Dear, you'll be perfect, stunning!" Jason laughed and kissed her.

"All I need is a matching necklace, something to make my outfit look chic. I think gold with precious stones would be right," she pleaded.

"Gold with precious stones? But darling, surely, you can use what you've got?"

She snuggled up to him, and whispered, "I want something stylish, to make you proud."

"But we can't afford that right now," he said, and went back to reading his book.

There was silence for a while.

"I've got an idea. I'll ask Lady Sophie to lend me one of hers," she said, her face lighting up.

***

Abbey looked at herself in the mirror, swirled around and smiled approvingly. She looked elegant in her tasteful outfit, with Lady Sophie's white gold, diamond necklace, enhancing her graceful neck. Her blond layered bob hairstyle accentuated the matching earrings.

Jason, her husband, tall and slender, with grey streaks in his dark hair, was dressed in a morning suit and waistcoat. Abbey adjusted his tie and commented on how distinguished he looked.

Their expressions were of a couple in love. They left the apartment and kissed in the lift.

***

Jason handed the invitation to one of the Garden Party Ladies. Abbey and Jason strolled arm-in-arm through the garden, chatted with other guests and listened to the military bands playing 60s songs.

"Pinch me, darling. This feels like a dream. Look at that

buffet table inside the main marquee," Abbey said, her eyes shone with delight.

The staff poured tea and cordial drinks to the guests. They helped themselves to salmon sandwiches, scones, strawberry tartlets.

When the Royal family stepped out onto the terrace, the National Anthem played. The Queen walked towards them, accompanied by her 'Senior Usher'. Abbey could tell that something was wrong, judging by Jason's peculiar reaction. He grabbed Abbey's arm and attempted to steer her away. Abbey wouldn't have any of that, she wanted to meet the Queen.

"Abbey, I know this man. I don't want to embarrass him," he apologised, but too late.

"Your Majesty. Let me introduce you to Mr and Mrs Farrell. Jason Farrell is a member of the High Court. Abbey, his wife, devotes her time to the charitable trust for the homeless."

Jason and Abbey greeted the Queen and made polite conversation. Jason and the elderly man exchanged words. Abbey sensed an anxious suspense between the two men and wondered if they were keeping something quiet.

Abbey enjoyed the Royal Garden Party and was sorry when three hours later, the National Anthem played again, signalling the end of the event.

As they left, Abbey asked her husband, "The Usher seemed to know you. Who is he?"

"He's Retired Major Douglas McGinn, an old friend and colleague of my father. They were in the same Regiment in the Army, for several years," Jason replied, sounding tense.

***

The following day, Abbey visited Lady Sophie to return the jewellery she'd borrowed.

Lady Sophie served Darjeeling tea and Victoria sponge

cake in the parlour.

"Did you have a nice time, my dear?" Lady Sophie sounded interested.

"Yes, it was better than I expected," replied Abbey. "Thank you for trusting me with your necklace and earrings. They must have cost a fortune. I'm glad I returned them intact," said Abbey, with relief.

"They weren't expensive, made from silver with quartz stones. My husband gave me the set on our wedding day. I've always liked those, so they're of sentimental value," Lady Sophie said, her eyes wrinkled in a smile.

"Neither gold nor diamonds? They look like it," Abbey was astonished.

"Abbey, I don't believe we can buy ourselves into the world of refinement. It doesn't work that way. Classiness is something that comes from the inside of a person and through education," said Lady Sophie, looking warmly at Abbey.

After they'd chatted for a while, Abbey realised that this conversation had shown a different Lady Sophie to the one she knew. She discovered that when she had come of age, she'd travelled the world, met people from different backgrounds and eventually spoke several languages.

Abbey noticed a photo of Lady Sophie and her deceased husband, taken at the height of his career. Lord Thomas wore his Army uniform. The photo showed a man, with a curled moustache and a cheerful face. Lady Sophie was shorter than her husband and wavy, dark hair framed her suntanned face. There seemed to be a real harmony between them.

"You look such a happy couple, Lady Sophie," said Abbey, putting the photo back on the shelf.

Lady Sophie's expression changed, and the glimpse into the past reflected in her eyes.

Abbey saw another photo of a young soldier, and asked, "Does your son visit you often?"

"That's George. My husband and I couldn't have

children, so we looked after him."

"He's good-looking," said Abbey.

Lady Sophie nodded, drew a deep breath, and composed herself.

"George was my husband's brother's son. Douglas had a glorious career as soldier ahead of him, but after his wife, Alice died, he had a nervous breakdown. Douglas asked us to look after his son, George," she cleared her voice. "Alice was an eccentric young woman, raising eyebrows and attracting critical comments in our circles. She was pretty, witty and gifted. Douglas adored her."

Lady Sophie picked up the photo and looked deep in thought.

"When George was eighteen, he joined the Army, like his father, Major Douglas McGinn. George died during an attack on mission in Afghanistan. He was a brave soldier and a Major, the image of his father," her voice broke.

They were interrupted by the phone ringing.

"I need to take this call," Lady Sophie apologised.

'Major Douglas McGinn,' thought Abbey. 'That explains the silence between the two men.'

Abbey reflected on the day before, filled with such happiness and joy.

When they said goodbye, Lady Sophie kissed Abbey's cheek.

"Thank you, Lady Sophie. I'll never forget this," said Abbey. "Yesterday may have looked like paradise, but after having heard your story, I realise that the reality isn't always what it appears to be."

32
THE POND
By Linda Nash

Madeleine sat at her kitchen table, enjoying a cup of tea. She looked out of the kitchen window, which faced on to her narrow back garden. It had finally stopped raining, the sun had come out, and the sky had turned a brilliant blue with little wisps of snowy white cloud racing across it. Even her overgrown garden looked shiny and new. Madeleine thought back to when Fred, her husband, was alive and how the garden had been full of flowers; daffodils and tulips in the Spring, antirrhinums, sweet peas and geraniums in the summer and dahlias of every variety and colour, in the Autumn. After his death she had tried to keep the garden together, but in the end she had given up and left it to the weeds. But that was such a long time ago. She sighed and brought her mind back firmly to the present. Today was just the day for a walk. She looked down at her flowered dress. Yes, that would do. No need for a cardigan. A voice cut through her thoughts,

"I'll be off now, Mrs. Phillips, if you're sure there's nothing else you want doing. See you this evening."

Madeleine nodded and listened until she heard Mrs Hughes start her car and drive away. She finished her tea, left her cup on the table and picked up her handbag. She glanced in the hall mirror, making sure her hair was tidy, and opened the kitchen door, remembering to pick up her walking stick. The birds were singing and the air felt warm. Madeleine opened the garden gate and walked slowly down the street.

One of the neighbours called to her. "Hello Madeleine, it's lovely to see you out and about again."

Madeleine glanced at him, smiled and walked on. Arriving at the main road, she carefully made her way across the zebra crossing and ten minutes later was in front of the park gates. She headed across the park in the direction of the pond, making her way through throngs of people, enjoying the unseasonable weather. There were children racing about on bikes, roller skates and scooters, mothers pushing prams and pushchairs, young men and women, and some not so young, jogging, while others just sat, enjoying the warm sunshine.

Oh good, her favourite bench was free, the one facing the pond. She went to it as quickly as she could, and sat down, looking around her. Somehow, it looked different, and she tried to think why. Oh, of course the pond had been made into a children's paddling pool. It was a good idea and probably more useful, but the pond had once been beautiful. There were different coloured goldfish, some of them quite big, and in the early summer the pond was covered in water lilies. Madeleine watched the children, splashing in the shallow water, carefully watched by their anxious looking mothers. She looked up, someone was asking her something,

"Do you mind if I sit here?" Madeleine smiled and nodded and the young woman sat down, holding a squirming toddler on her lap. The little boy looked curiously at Madeleine, touching her arm with his podgy fingers. She caressed them gently and he chuckled and grinned at her.

"Oh, I'm sorry," said the young woman. "He's always

doing that." She took him to the edge of the pool, where he sat and splashed happily, looking up at his mother from time to time.

When his clothes were soaking, the little boy was persuaded to leave the pool. His mother dried and changed him and then strapped him into his pushchair, all the time protesting noisily. She said goodbye to Madeleine and pushed him, still shouting, in the direction of the park gates.

Shortly afterwards, Madeleine was aware of someone else sitting next to her. She looked around to see a young man, eating sandwiches. Glancing at the pool, she saw that most of the children had left. She thought about moving to another bench, but didn't because she felt quite comfortable where she was. The man eventually finished his sandwiches, threw the wrappings in the bin and strode off.

Madeleine became aware of more people around her. There were several boys dressed in sailor suits and carrying boats. Others were sailing their boats on the pond, with the help of long sticks. Little girls were shouting encouragement to their brothers, while parents and possibly nannies were sitting on chairs around the pond, keeping a watchful eye on their charges. There was a loud quacking as one of the boats sailed too close to a duck. A small boy with dark hair started to wail, when he realised he could no longer reach his boat. Madeleine leaned forward. Surely, that was her younger brother, Daniel. He waded in after his boat, but one of the adults quickly pulled him out.

'Goodness,' thought Madeleine, 'it's my father.'

She tried to speak to him, but he didn't appear to hear her. A few minutes later, she noticed that her brother had returned to the pond when he realised that his father was reading his newspaper and he was wading in more quickly this time. Suddenly, he must have caught his foot on something, as he fell over and almost disappeared.

Madeleine leaped to her feet and ran towards the pond shouting, and she quickly waded in and reached where her brother was lying. She saw her father beside her, as he scooped up her brother, taking him away from the pond. There was a little girl, with dark hair and a pretty flowered dress, standing on the edge, crying. 'Why that's me,' she thought. Meanwhile, her father had taken the limp body of her brother and laid him on the grass and was trying to revive him. Another man came running over to them, holding a black bag. He took out a stethoscope and bent over Daniel, examining him. He eventually stood up and slowly shook his head. Both Madeleine and her younger self were standing there, looking at the inert body of their brother, weeping. Her father was bent over Daniel, helplessly wringing his hands, tears running down his face.

She woke with a start aware of someone shaking her. A man in uniform was standing over her. Goodness, it was almost dark and she felt so cold. She shivered.

"Are you alright, Madam? I was doing my rounds before closing the gates for the night, and I noticed you sitting there crying," he said. "You must be cold with just that thin dress."

Madeleine wiped the tears away with her hand, smiled at him and tried to explain, but he couldn't seem to hear her. She slowly got to her feet. She stood there for several moments, leaning heavily on her stick, trying to get rid of the stiffness in her legs and back. She followed the park keeper to the gates, which he locked behind them.

"Will you be able to get home, love," he asked her. "Is there anyone I can phone for you?"

Madeleine shook her head and walked away in the direction of home. She had been walking for some time when she realised that she didn't seem to be any nearer home, although it rarely took her that long. She stopped, looking around to see if she recognised anything. 'Balfour Street.' She wracked her brain, trying to remember if she knew the name. But, it was no good, it didn't seem familiar at all.

Madeleine stood there for several minutes, but felt so cold she thought she had better keep moving. She should have brought her cardigan, but it was warm when she left home, and she hadn't felt the need. She remembered her mother saying when she was young, 'better safe than sorry'. It made her think of her dead brother again and she felt tears pricking at the back of her eyes.

Just when she couldn't think what she was going to do, a policeman appeared out of the gloom. He stopped when he saw Madeleine peering at the street name.

"You lost, love?" he asked.

Madeleine tried to answer him, but when she realised that he could not hear what she was trying to say, she nodded.

"Have you got your address?" he asked, pointing at her bag. Madeleine smiled with relief and handed him her bag.

The policeman opened it, going carefully through the contents. He pulled out an old address book, and there, on the first page, was the name and address of the owner. When he showed it to her she smiled and nodded.

The policeman took out his telephone, punched in a number, and asked the person at the other end if there was a squad car in the area, explaining that he had come across a lady, who was lost and who needed to get home as soon as possible.

He put his phone away and smiled at Madeleine. "They'll be along in a minute," he said. "Apparently, you'd been reported missing, and they were out looking for you."

'Oh, that must have been Mrs. Hughes,' thought Madeleine. 'Now she'll start going on that I'm not safe and it's time they put me in a home.'

In a few minutes, the police car arrived and the policeman helped her into the back seat. Shortly afterwards they arrived at Madeleine's house and she could see Mrs. Hughes standing in the doorway. Mrs Hughes rushed down the path and helped Madeleine out of the car. She then tried to take hold of her arm, but Madeleine pushed her away. 'She was quite capable of walking up the path on her own, thank you.'

Feeling stiff from all her walking, she leaned heavily on her stick as she walked up the path, with Mrs. Hughes tut tutting behind her. "You might have been run over, out there all on your own, to say nothing of catching your death of cold. Why, you haven't even got a cardigan on and it's the beginning of October." She finished with the inevitable, "Not being able to speak any more puts you in danger. You really will have to go in a home, if you keep doing this sort of thing."

Madeleine let her words wash over her. She had heard a version of this so many times. 'Yes she was old, yes she did have lapses of memory and people didn't seem to hear what she was saying any more, but was that a reason to take her away from her home, where she had lived all her married life. Not that she had been married very long, she thought sadly, her husband Fred had been killed near the end of the war. Then she could have done with being looked after, when she had lost the baby on hearing the news about Fred. The tears slipped from under her eyelids, running slowly down her cheeks.

Mrs Hughes stopped ranting when she saw that Madeleine was crying. She was not an unkind woman, but considered the elderly to be rather like children. They should do as they were told by those who knew better. She went over to Madeleine and put her arms around her. "There, there, you go and sit on the settee. I'll get a blanket to put around you and make you a nice cup of tea."

She left when Madeleine was safely tucked up in bed, promising to be back, first thing in the morning. The old lady fell asleep at once, tired out by the excitement of her day.

But, where was she? She appeared to be in a sitting room, no she wasn't, it was the front parlour. Over there was her mother, wearing a black hat with a veil over her face and a long, black, lacy dress. She was clasping a lace handkerchief in her hand, with which she kept dabbing her eyes. Her father, too, was wearing a black suit, and wasn't that her grandmother sitting hunched on a chair in the corner of the room? She looked down at herself. She, too, was wearing a black dress, with stockings and shoes to match. All at once it came to her. Of course, her brother had drowned. She looked across the room and there against the far wall was her brother's coffin.

Hesitantly, Madeleine walked towards it. Her brother was lying there, dressed in his sailor suit. He looked as though he was sleeping, but his skin was pale and waxy looking. As she looked at him, his eyes opened and he looked up at her and smiled. Madeleine put her hand over her mouth in shock and looked to see if anybody had noticed. He beckoned to her to climb into the coffin. Madeleine looked around to see if anyone was watching, but the grownups seemed to be engaged in conversation, so she climbed onto the chair and into the coffin.

Daniel grabbed her hand. The bottom of the coffin fell away and they were running down a long, winding, staircase. As they neared the bottom, the light was so bright that Madeleine had to shade her eyes. When she looked up, she saw stretching in front of her vast, grassy meadow, studded with brightly coloured wild flowers. In the distance was a group of people, who seemed to be waving to them.

"Come on," said her brother. "They're waiting for us."

Madeleine hesitated for a moment. Did she really want to join them? But then, on the other hand, what did she have to lose? Madeleine felt a great surge of happiness. Laughing with joy, she took Daniel's hand again and together they ran across the grass.

33
TRY TO FORGET
By Vesla Small

'Oh, my God,' she thought.

The man lying on the ground looked at Turid, he moaned in distress. His body bled from welts that reminded her of a whipping. The man gazed at her with wild eyes. His chin and cheekbones stuck out, and his tall body looked famished.

Turid looked around in panic wondering what she could do.

Russians, taken by the Gestapo as prisoners of war, had been seen in the area. It was common knowledge that if they were caught, they would be sent back to Russia and treated as traitors. She needed to find a hiding place for him while she looked for a solution.

Turid helped the man to stand, held him around his waist whilst he put his arm over her shoulder. Together, they moved tortuously towards the earth cave. Once they were outside the shelter, she assisted the man to sit on a boulder.

"Spasiba," he said, and looked at her with a weak smile.

Turid smiled back, and replied, "You're welcome."

She walked to the river, where she soaked her

headscarf in the water. Whilst she cleaned the man's wounds, she hummed a Russian song that her grandfather learnt from a Russian shipmate, "Kalinka, kalinka, kalinka moya."

A tear ran down his cheek. "Minya zavoot Vladimir," he said, took her hand, and kissed it as a mark of respect.

"I'm Turid," she answered, a smile rising on her lips.

Turid wondered if there was anything left of the food stored in the shelter, her fiancé's place of escape from the Gestapo, and if the woollen blankets were still there.

When she opened the small door into the cave, a stench of humidity and rot hit her. She opened the door to let in fresh air. Huddled over, she went inside the turf hut, where she found a jar of beans, which she opened and offered to Vladimir, who wolfed it down.

Although the war was over, her mother seemed on constant watch, so Turid needed to get home before they came looking for her. When she helped Vladimir into the refuge, she felt him push an envelope into her hand, which she accepted without comment.

The winter was giving way to the spring, and between the snow patches, bits of vegetation appeared. The sound of the rippling rivers made Turid feel calm. She was on her way home, three weeks after peace was declared on 8th May 1945.

When Turid walked into the kitchen, her parents were waiting for her, and her mother asked if she'd met anybody. Turid didn't want to worry them unnecessarily and answered, "No." In silence, she left the room and climbed the stairs leading to her bedroom.

The envelope was sealed and addressed to her. Turid was puzzled how a Russian prisoner of war could be the courier of a letter from England. It was apparent that he'd been looking for her, and she wondered whether he was an ally or an enemy. Turid slit the envelope open with a penknife and glanced over the letter. To her relief, it was written in Norwegian.

Turid sat on the side of the bed and read the letter. Her eyebrows rose at first, followed by anger, then she sobbed quietly, clutching her handkerchief.

'To spy for the Nazis, and imprisoned in Russia,' Turid looked sombre. That made little sense, and that wasn't the Svein she knew.

The content of the letter was unbelievable, and Turid read it again and again. According to the letter, the incident happened after the last sabotage attack against the Germans. Svein and another Resistance member fled to Russia, from where a fishing vessel would take them to England. The two men had been interrogated in Murmansk by the NKGB, People's Commissariat for State Security. They were accused of being spies and put in a prison camp. Somebody must have denounced them, but who?

Turid was heartbroken and wondered how such injustice could happen. Her immediate thought was 'the messenger', and she promised herself that this wouldn't go unpunished.

***

It was midnight, everybody was in bed and the house was quiet. Turid crept down the stairs, avoiding the squeaky steps. After searching under the boards of the kitchen floor, she found what she was looking for. She gripped the rifle her father had hidden from the Gestapo and wrapped it into an old blanket. With the hood of her anorak pulled over her head, she slid out of the house carrying the rifle across her body. It was overcast, which made it easier for her to walk unnoticed in a land illuminated by the midnight sun.

The letter was on her mind as she trudged along the forest path. Turid glanced around and behind her now and then to make sure no one followed her and jumped at the sound of a rock ptarmigan fluttering its wings. When she opened the small door to the refuge where she'd left Vladimir, she looked at him sombrely, then lifted the rifle and pointed it at him.

Vladimir, wrapped in a blanket, looked as if he was in meditation. When he heard Turid, he opened his eyes and looked at her with relief.

Turid sensed that he was expecting her.

"Spasiba," he said. Removing the blanket, he climbed out of the shelter.

Why Vladimir thanked her, she couldn't understand. After all, she was pointing the rifle at him. Maybe he didn't know what was written in the letter. She was unable to think straight. Besides, she'd never used a gun.

When Turid aimed the rifle to his chest, shivers went down her back. As she brushed her finger along the trigger to get the feel of it, her palm felt wet. The panic overtook her, and she lowered the rifle, looking into his eyes. Vladimir seemed unafraid and ready for death, which made it even more difficult for her, but she had to do it. Her lips curved, and she regained self-control. Once more, she pointed the muzzle of the rifle at his heart, imagining it exploding when the bullet ravaged it. Holding her finger on the trigger until her sight was on target, she squeezed it. The sound of the shot echoed, and the back blast of the gun nearly took her off her feet.

Vladimir let out a plaintive moan and fell.

Paralysed, Turid was unable to move and to think. She laid the weapon on the ground, sat on the boulder where Vladimir had sat hours before. Thinking was worse than physical pain. As she wiped her eyes, she sobbed.

***

In her peripheral vision, she saw something behind her. As she turned around, she gasped.

"Johan, what are you doing here?" Turid whispered.

A cold chill crept down her spine. Johan was a Nazi

supporter. After peace was declared, he'd gone. Rumours had it he'd committed suicide for fear of the punishment awaiting him as a collaborator.

"That bullet should have been for me, and not him," said Johan.

"Yes Johan. Vladimir was most likely a better man than you, but he had to go," she sounded distant and hard, pursing her lips in disdain, as she reached for her father's rifle.

"Pull the trigger," Johan pleaded.

Turid hesitated. How could she? Johan was twenty-one, the same age as her. They'd gone to the same school, played and had fun together, until this poisonous war separated them, in 1940. Sigrid, Svein, Johan and Turid had been the best of friends. Where did it go wrong?

It had saddened Turid when the Germans killed Sigrid in July '43. After the German invasion in April '40, several people escaped to Russia. Instead of the long, hazardous voyage by sea to England, they chose the shorter distance to Russia. Although many were communists, they were still good Norwegians. Their intention was to continue their fight to liberate their country from there, and Sigrid's brother was one of them. When the Gestapo unravelled the partisans' network, the situation became dangerous for the supporters. Sigrid was part of the assistants the partisans relied on to provide information to the Allies about the Germans in Norway. Turid was remorseful when thinking about the waste of a good Norwegian patriot and a dear friend.

For nearly five years, she'd shared the secret of Svein being part of the Resistance. Despite the Gestapo's infiltration and destruction, the movement survived and continued to grow. It had been difficult for her and the family during the German occupation, always fearing the Gestapo's 'knock on the door'. Svein had taken part in one of the Norwegian Resistance's latest sabotage actions after which he'd escaped to the mountains. Turid wondered whether Svein was a part of the Resistance or a German spy, although it made no difference, now that the war was over. She still loved him and worried about Svein, whose child she was expecting.

Turid stood facing Johan, her friend from the past. She was mystified how the war had divided the four school friends, a friendship based on trust, loyalty and affection. Not in her wildest dreams could she imagine that each of them would have such different fates in life. Turid no longer trusted Johan, she despised him. As she studied Johan's long pointed nose and pale face, she wondered why Johan was begging her to put an end to his life.

"Johan, you watched them burn our homes, slaughter our livestock and sink our fishing boats. You saw them kill the partisans. They killed Sigrid, our best friend. You prospered when partisans suffered and risked their lives for the sake of our country. How could you?" her voice trembled.

"Why should I shoot you, Johan? Tell me!" she was angry, with her eyes on fire she stared at him accusingly.

Johan explained, tears running down his cheeks. He'd tried to rescue Sigrid, when he transported her and other partisans over the bay, in his fishing boat. He'd tried to hide them from the enemy, but had failed.

"Why did you betray your friends, your country?" Turid asked.

"My family was poor. Tuberculosis killed my father before the war. To feed and care for eight children during the war was a huge burden on my mother. I was the eldest of the siblings, so when the Germans offered me work, I couldn't refuse. We were starving," he looked away.

"I cannot continue to live, knowing I've betrayed my people and my country," Johan sounded desperate, his shoulders stooped, he looked shattered.

Turid stared into his eyes. "Nine of the forty five heroic partisans survived that day. Only nine, Johan!" Turid pointed the rifle against his forehead.

There was a mixture of desperation and relief on Johan's face.

"Please, do it... Now," he pleaded.

Her thoughts went to the letter that Vladimir gave her, prompting apprehension. Svein in a 'friendly' country's prison camp accused of spying for Germany. That was crazy. She was confused.

Turid stood, holding the rifle, when she heard someone tramping through the thicket, and a familiar voice shouting, "Don't shoot. Johan's a Partisan."

***

Turid turned around, and couldn't believe who would walk towards them.

"Father? Mother?" she said, stunned.

"Johan's a partisan," repeated her father.

'Pigs might fly,' thought Turid, looking at her father in disbelief.

She struggled to believe that Johan was a partisan. He'd been a collaborator, working for the Nazis ever since the war started, and the Quislings helped the Germans to find the partisans and those who'd been hiding them.

"First, you betray us and then you defend us. What kind of morality is that?" she confronted Johan.

"That's what they'll say about us, now that the war is finished. Whether we've been a collaborator or a partisan, they won't regard us as good Norwegian citizens. Both will be looked upon as traitors," Johan roared.

Johan's comment baffled Turid, unaware that was how people felt about the partisans and their supporters, whom she'd considered as defenders of their freedom.

She regained her poise. This was not the moment to be upset about mistakes. Nothing could change the past.

***

Her mother took the rifle from Turid, looked at her daughter, and whispered, "That's my girl, fearless."

When her mother looked to where Vladimir's dead body lay, her face looked lifeless, like a closed door.

Turid's insides knotted as she watched her tired looking parents. She'd never seen them this way. They had been lucky to survive the war, its hardships and humiliations, and this was thanks to her parents who never gave up.

Facing her parents, Turid realised how much they had aged. Her mother's shoulders were thin, her eyes sagged and her posture showed a worn out woman of barely fifty. Her father looked no better, although an 'iron man', the lack of food and hardship during the war had made him a shadow of what he once was.

The war was a tragic and painful part in everyone's life. It tore families, friends and sweethearts apart, and many people were homeless. The awful experiences were haunting her with nightmares, angst and flashbacks. When she spoke about this to her parents, they kept saying, "Just try to forget." But how could she forget the horrors of this war, especially the inhumane treatment of the prisoners of war? How could she forget the many times when 'Jerry' had killed her compatriots, who chose not to evacuate, but hid and fought?

All they longed for was to live in peace in a free country. Instead, the war had made Finnmark into a melting pot of horrors, disappearances and misunderstandings.

Turid looked at her parents, studying their sorrowful expressions. She thought about her brother, Baard, who'd lost his life, walking on a landmine. His loss had an impact on all of them, especially her father, with Baard being the only son.

***

Her mind switched back to the present confusing

situation, with Vladimir, the Russian prisoner of war's dead body, Johan, her two-faced friend from the past and herself, all of them guarded by her parents, who had aged prematurely.

The couple crouched, lifted the corpse, put it into the turf hut and closed the door.

Her father held the rifle. Restraining the barking dog, her mother walked towards Johan and took him by his arm.

Her mother's eyes shone with tears, as she looked at her daughter, saying, "We'll find Johan a shelter."

Then she walked towards her husband, saying, "It's best to hide Johan in the summer cow barn."

Her husband nodded, and they walked towards the pastures in the highland.

Turid stood watching the three people disappear behind the hillock.

It was morning, and the sun shone through the clouds. As Turid laid her hand on her abdomen, she felt the baby move inside her. Her lips curled into a smile, she felt appeased, as thoughts of kindness and forgiveness ran through her. She looked forward to bringing up their child in a free country.

A shot interrupted her thoughts followed by silence. Half an hour later, Turid saw two shapes coming over the horizon.

Would you please consider leaving a review of 'Signposts' on Amazon?

Thank you.

www.casteau-scribblers.com